'Deserves three cheers . . . the most richly
enjoyable Wilson novel for years'
The Times

♥

'As a piece of escapism, it's a glorious,
book-length version of one of the
photo-stories in *Jackie* magazine'
Observer

♥

'Wilson treats this subject with
extraordinary emotional intelligence'
Mail on Sunday

♥

'Jacqueline Wilson is particularly good
at putting herself inside the skin of
awkward misfit characters'
Spectator

♥

'A hard-hitting and compulsively
readable tale for teenagers'
Irish Independent

♥

'Jacqueline Wilson at her very best'
Publishing News

♥

'This catalogue of troubles is handled
deftly, wittily and sensitively'
Irish Sunday Independent

www.kidsatrandomhouse.co.uk

Join the official Jacqueline Wilson fan club at
www.jacquelinewilson.co.uk

JACQUELINE WILSON

Love
Lessons

Illustrated by Nick Sharratt

CORGI BOOKS

LOVE LESSONS
A CORGI BOOK 978 0 552 55352 0 (from January 2007)
0 552 55352 2

First published in Great Britain by Doubleday,
an imprint of Random House Children's Books

Doubleday edition published 2005
Corgi edition published 2006

1 3 5 7 9 10 8 6 4 2

Papers used by Random House Children's Books are natural,
recyclable products made from wood grown in sustainable forests.
The manufacturing processes conform to the environmental
regulations of the country of origin.

Corgi Books are published by Random House Children's Books,
61–63 Uxbridge Road, London W5 5SA,
a division of The Random House Group Ltd,
in Australia by Random House Australia (Pty) Ltd,
20 Alfred Street, Milsons Point, Sydney, NSW 2061, Australia,
in New Zealand by Random House New Zealand Ltd,
18 Poland Road, Glenfield, Auckland 10, New Zealand,
and in South Africa by Random House (Pty) Ltd,
Isle of Houghton, Corner of Boundary Road & Carse O'Gowrie,
Houghton 2198, South Africa

THE RANDOM HOUSE GROUP Limited Reg. No. 954009
www.kidsatrandomhouse.co.uk

A CIP catalogue record for this book is available from the British Library.

Printed and bound in Great Britain by
Bookmarque Ltd, Croydon, Surrey

For Mary, Rachel and Rebecca

I hate my dad.

I know lots of teenage girls say that but they don't really mean it. Well, I don't *think* they do. I don't really know any other teenage girls. That's one of the reasons why I hate Dad. He keeps me a virtual prisoner.

I'm interrogated if I slip down the road to Krisha's Korner Shop. I'm not allowed to go into town by myself. I can't go to see any films. I can't eat in McDonald's.

Dad even fussed about me making a simple bus ride by myself to go to Miss Roberts for maths tuition. He took my sister Grace and me out of school ages ago, when I'd just gone into the Juniors and she was still at the finger-painting stage. Dad said *he* was going to educate us.

We were left to get on with it for ages, but this summer we had a home visit from a Mr Miles, who was from some kind of education authority. He wanted to know what provision Dad was making for my GCSE coursework. Dad said he didn't believe in examinations. Mr Miles smiled through Dad's tirade, obviously having heard it all before. He looked at Grace and me when Dad ran out of steam.

'What do you want to do when you're older, Prudence and Grace?' he asked.

Grace mumbled something about working with animals. Dad won't let us have any proper pets because he says he's allergic to them. Grace has a lot of secret, unsatisfactory pets, like the blackbird in the garden and the toads in the compost heap and for a while she kept a wormery hidden under her bed. Grace's pets are not exactly cuddly.

'You'll certainly need to pass lots of exams if you want to be a vet,' said Mr Miles.

Dad snorted. 'You'll find our Grace has got no more brains than a donkey,' he said unkindly. 'She'll get a job in a shop somewhere and be happy enough.'

'In your bookshop?'

'She can help sell the books, but I doubt she's up to the business side of things,' said Dad. 'But Prudence can do all the cataloguing and buying and book fairs.'

'Is that what you want to do, Prudence – run your father's business?' said Mr Miles.

2

I swallowed. 'I – I'd like to go to art college,' I said.

Dad glared at me. 'For goodness' sake, I've told you to forget that nonsense. You don't need to go away to college to learn drawing and painting; you can do that already.'

'But I *want* to go, Dad.'

Dad was furious with me for arguing in front of Mr Miles, but decided not to pursue it. 'All right, all right, go to art college, waste three years, see for yourself,' he said. He nodded triumphantly at Mr Miles. 'I guarantee she can pass her art GCSE standing on her head.'

'I dare say,' said Mr Miles. 'But I think you'll find art colleges require quite a few GCSEs, plus three good A-levels. You're going to have to make more provision for your daughters' education, Mr King, especially now Prudence is fourteen. Otherwise we might have to pursue the matter through the courts.'

'The courts!' said Mum, panicking.

'You've got no power to do any such thing,' said Dad, hands on his hips, his chin jutting. 'You can't stop parents home-educating their children.'

'Not if they've been home-educated right from the start. But your girls have attended school in the past, so I think you'll find we have every power. However, let's hope we can avoid any unpleasant action. We all want what's best for Prudence and Grace.'

Dad seemed sure Mr Miles was bluffing, but

nevertheless he fixed up for me to go to this Miss Roberts for maths tuition on Wednesday afternoons.

I only went once. It was unbearable.

Miss Roberts used to teach maths at a girls' school way back in the sixties. She seemed preserved in that time, still teasing her limp grey hair into a bouffant style. Her pink scalp showed through alarmingly. I kept staring at it as she bent over me, trying to explain some supposedly simple point about algebra.

I couldn't understand any of it. I wrote down random letters of the alphabet but I couldn't tease any meaning from them. I expect letters to arrange themselves into words. If I'm doing sums I need numbers – though I'm actually useless with numbers too. I can't always add up accurately. The shop takings rarely balance on a Saturday when I help out.

Miss Roberts tried hard to be patient with me. She explained it over and over again, raising her voice and speaking very s-l-o-w-l-y. Then she switched to geometry in despair. I could draw wobbly circles with her old compass and construct reasonable squares and rectangles with my own ruler but I didn't know what any of them *meant*.

I paid her the twenty pounds for the tuition and she gave me a cup of tea (the milk was so old it floated in little flecks on the tan surface) and a stale custard cream.

'Don't look so woebegone, Prudence,' she said.

4

'Your father says you're a very bright girl. I'm sure you'll catch on in no time.'

I made an extreme effort to swallow the sour milk-biscuity paste in my mouth and thanked her politely.

I didn't go back. For the last three Wednesdays I've walked into town and spent my tuition fee. Sixty whole pounds.

I've never had so much money in my life before. Dad gives Grace and me one pound every Saturday. He behaves as if he's bestowing solid gold upon us, and even has the nerve to lecture us, telling us not to waste it on rubbish. I've always saved mine up to buy sketchpads and soft pencils and coloured crayons, bought one by one.

Grace spends hers all at once on sweets – a bar of chocolate or two, and a handful of gummy snakes. She gollops the chocolate in one go but she keeps the snakes, lining them up on the arm of the sofa, red and yellow and green like a slithery traffic light. She plays with them, giving them names and personalities, but she can't help licking them affectionately so that they all get very sticky. She tries to save them till Sunday, though she sometimes can't stop herself biting off a head or two on Saturday night.

Grace isn't three or four, as you might expect. She is eleven years old and very weird.

I know I am very weird too. I can't seem to help it. I don't know how to be a proper teenager. I bought a couple of teenage magazines out of my stolen tuition money. They were astonishing, especially the problem pages. I knew I didn't look anything like girls my own age, but I didn't realize my experiences were so different.

I've had *no* experiences; *they've* had plenty. The girls writing to the problem pages spoke a different language and behaved as if they were from a totally different planet. They wore astonishing clothes and got up to astonishing things with their boyfriends. I read these letters feeling hot, my heart beating.

The only letters I could identify with in any way were the ones where the girls moaned about their mums and dads. They said they couldn't stick their parents. Their mums wouldn't let them have a nose stud or platform heels; their dads nagged about bad marks at school and got mad if they didn't come home till midnight.

'They should try having *my* mum and dad,' I muttered, as I flicked through them by torchlight under the bedcovers.

'What?' Grace said blearily, propping herself up on one elbow. 'Are you still awake? What are you doing?'

'Just reading my book. Go back to sleep,' I said.

But Grace has bat ears. She heard the rustle of the pages. 'That's not a book, it's a magazine! Let me see!' She leaned over from her bed. She leaned far too eagerly and fell out with a yell.

'Shut *up*, Grace!'

'Ouch! I've banged my elbow – and my knee!' Grace whimpered.

'Ssh!'

'It hurts,' she whispered. She came scrabbling into my bed. 'Please let me see, Prue.'

'You won't tell Mum?' I hissed.

Grace sometimes has terrible attacks of conscience when she worries and frets about some tiny little thing she's done wrong and then suddenly blurts it all out to Mum when they're having a cuddle. Grace is far too big for cuddles now but she still wants them. She's like a large lollopy dog, desperate to be patted all the time.

I didn't waste my breath warning her not to tell Dad. Even Grace isn't that mad.

'I swear,' she said. Then she whispered all the worst words she knew, swearing like a trooper. We might live like princesses locked in a tower but you can't go down the street without hearing boys blinding away and drivers yelling. Also, very strangely, Dad sometimes swears when he's in one of his tempers, foul words frothing out of his mouth. If Mum or Grace or I ever said just one of those words he would murder us.

I showed Grace the magazines. She handled them reverently, as if they were the finest first folios, easing over the pages and smoothing them out. She looked at all the photos of teenage girls and stroked their clothes longingly. She started reading the problem page and then snorted with shocked laughter.

'Ssh!'

'What's this girl going *on* about? What does she *mean*?'

7

'Oh, for heaven's sake, Grace, you know the facts of life,' I said, although I wasn't clear what a lot of it meant either.

I had secretly looked at several volumes of Victorian erotica which Dad bought in a book auction, presumably by mistake. I found them right at the bottom of the box, under a Norton set of the Brontë sisters. They featured a bizarre vicar, Reverend Knightly, with a large congregation of ever so lusty ladies. There were extraordinary colour plates showing the vicar cavorting in his dog collar and very little else. I found them comical but not particularly disturbing. They were adults, figments of someone's imagination, and one hundred and fifty years old. The girls in these magazines were real.

'Oh I *wish* I had a boyfriend,' said Grace. 'Do you think Dad will ever let us go out with boys, Prue?'

'I don't *want* to go out with boys,' I said, not entirely truthfully.

For years and years I'd had a private pretend friend, an interesting and imaginative girl my own age called Jane. She started when I read the first few chapters of *Jane Eyre*. She stepped straight out of the pages and into my head. She no longer led her own Victorian life with her horrible aunt and cousins. She shared *my* life with my demented father.

Jane was better than a real sister. She wasn't babyish and boring like Grace. We discussed books and pored over pictures and painted watercolours together, and we talked endlessly about everything. Sometimes we didn't talk silently enough. I knew my lips moved and occasionally I started muttering without realizing. Grace knew I made up imaginary games inside my head and resented it.

'You're doing it!' she'd say when I muttered, giving me a nudge. 'Tell *me*, Prue, go on. Make it up for me.'

'Make up your own games,' I said, which was unfair, because she wasn't much good at it.

I'd started up a new and even more private pretend game recently, after Dad had taken Grace and me on an educational trip to the National Gallery in London. Dad had an old guidebook to the gallery and was all set to inform us relentlessly, but the gallery had long since rearranged all its rooms. Dad couldn't match up the text in his guidebook with any of the paintings and became more and more frustrated and irritable.

Grace barely looked at each painting, trudging with bent head, her feet dragging on the floor. She murmured obediently whenever Dad seemed to demand a response, but that was all.

I didn't say much either. I was flying through this new magical world of religious Renaissance painting, so pink and blue and glittery gold. It was as if I'd sprouted my own beautiful set of angels' wings. I'd always painted wings plain white, but now I saw they could be shaded from the palest pearl through deep rose and purple to the darkest midnight-blue tips. Some of the angels' wings were carefully co-ordinated with their gowns like matching accessories. Others had unusual, eccentric colour combinations like red and gold and black, with a white gown. One particular fashionista angel was strolling along the sandy path with a golden-haired boy about my age, holding a fish.

When we were little Dad used to read aloud to us every day from a large and unwieldy Victorian Bible. Dad had been very religious until he had a row with our vicar. He'd gently suggested to Dad that home-schooling was all very well, but Grace and I needed more of a social life so we could make some friends. Dad blew his top and had no time for the vicar, his church, or the entire Christian faith after that.

He put the Bible back on the shelves as stock. I was sorry when it sold, because I loved looking at the wonderful Doré illustrations. I remembered a lot of the Bible stories, so I knew that the boy with the fish and the angel friend was Tobias. He was dressed in colourful medieval garb, with dashing bright-red tights. I tried to imagine a modern teenage boy prancing about in scarlet stockings. Still, some boys wore their jeans skin-tight. The Tobias in the painting obligingly put on blue jeans and a white T-shirt and smiled at me.

He came home with me that day as my new imaginary friend. Poor Jane got elbowed into the background. Tobias and I read together, painted together, walked together, whispered together. He spoke softly right into my ear, his cheek very nearly brushing mine.

Now I imagined him kissing me, touching me, like the girls and their boyfriends in the magazines. But then I imagined real boys, with their foul mouths and grabbing hands, and I shuddered.

'I don't like boys,' I said.

'Boys like *you*, Prue,' said Grace. She sighed. 'It's not fair. I wish I was pretty like you so boys would turn round and stare at me.'

'I bet they only stare because I look such a freak,' I said.

Mum made most of our clothes from remnants from the Monday market stall. I'm fourteen years old and yet I have to wear demure little-girly dresses with short sleeves and swirly skirts. I have a red-and-white check, a baby blue with a little white flower motif, and a canary yellow piped with white. They are all embarrassingly awful.

Mum used to make appalling matching knickers when we were little, threaded with very unreliable elastic. Our baggy shop-bought white pants are only one degree better. Still, I have *proper* underwear now. I used my maths tuition money to buy a wonderful black bra with pink lace and a little pink rose, and two matching knickers, wispy little things a tenth of the size of my plain girls' pants.

I locked the bathroom and tried them on, standing precariously on the edge of the bath so I could peek at myself in the bathroom cabinet mirror. I loved the way they looked, the way they make *me* look.

I hadn't dared wear them yet under my awful dresses because Grace could so easily blab. I'd have to wash them out secretly myself rather than risk putting them in the laundry basket.

'Do we look like freaks?' Grace asked worriedly.

'Of course we do. Look at our clothes!'

Grace considered. 'I *like* my dresses, especially my pink one with the little panda pattern – it's so cute,' she said. 'Would you have liked that material for your dress, Prue?'

'No! I can't stick little pandas or teddies or bunny rabbits. For God's sake, I'm *fourteen*.'

'Do you think *I'm* too old to wear my panda dress?' Grace asked anxiously.

There was only one answer but I didn't want to upset her. 'I suppose your pink panda dress does still look quite sweet on you,' I lied valiantly.

'It's getting a bit small for me now anyway,' Grace sighed. '*All* my dresses are tight on me. I wish I wasn't getting so large and lumpy.'

'It's just a stage you go through. Puppy fat.'

'*You* didn't,' she sighed again. 'Dad keeps going on about me getting fat. He says I shouldn't eat so much. He says I'm greedy. Do you think I should go on a diet, Prue?'

'No! Take no notice of him. He just likes to nag, you know that. Anyway, you can't diet *just* yet. I've got you a surprise.'

12

I'd felt so mean spending all my tuition money on myself, though I knew Grace would never manage to keep any present I bought her properly hidden. The only way I could buy her a treat was to get her something edible, to be quickly consumed.

'A surprise!' said Grace, clapping her hands.

'Ssh! I was keeping it a secret, to cheer you up the next time Dad goes off on one of his rants, but you might as well have it now.'

I climbed out of bed and went to scrabble in my knicker drawer. My hands found the flimsy satin and lace of my new underwear. I secretly stroked them in the dark, and then searched again until my fingers slid over the crackly cellophane of Grace's surprise.

'OK! Here we are!' I slipped back into bed and thrust my present into her hands.

'What *is* it?' she said, unable to see properly in the dark.

I flicked the torch on to show her.

'Oh *wow*!'

'Shut *up*! Do you want Dad to hear?' I said, nudging her.

'Sorry. But, oh Prue, it's so *sweet*!'

There's a special chocolate boutique in the shopping centre. It's Grace's all-time favourite shop even though she's never even set foot inside it. Mum buys chocolate off a market stall. It's always a funny make and past its sell-by date, but it's cheap, and that's all Mum cares about.

I was going to buy Grace a pound of posh

chocolates in a fancy box, but then I saw this big white chocolate bunny in the window, clutching an orange marzipan carrot. I knew she'd love it.

'What shall I call him? Peter Rabbit? Benjamin Bunny?'

'Can't you ever make up your *own* names, Grace?'

'You know I can't. *You* think up a lovely name for him.'

'There's not much point. You'll be chomping away at him in two seconds. Knowing you, there won't even be a little chocolate paw left by midnight.'

'I'm not going to eat him. He's far too wonderful. I'm going to keep him for ever,' said Grace, but her fat little fingers had already undone his ribbon and peeled off his cellophane. She sniffed his creamy ears ecstatically. 'Oh, he smells heavenly!'

'So eat him, silly. That's what he's for.'

'I *can't*! Well, perhaps I could eat his carrot? I don't want to spoil him. Still, maybe I could just lick one of his ears, to see what he tastes like?'

'Go for it, girl!'

Grace stuck out her tongue and licked. And licked again and again and again. And then all by themselves her teeth started chomping and the chocolate bunny was left disturbingly hard of hearing.

'Oooh!' Grace murmured blissfully. Then she shone the torch on him. She saw what she'd done. '*Oooh!*' she wailed, her tone changing.

14

'It's OK, just eat his head up quickly. It's what he's *for*.'

'But it's *spoiling* him. Why am I such a greedy guts? Look, he's got a horrible gap in his head now.'

'He's fine.'

'No he's not. I want him to be whole again,' Grace said, looking as if she might burst into tears.

'Well, his ears are in your tummy. If you gobble up the rest of him quickly then his body can join up with them, and they can squidge themselves together like plasticine. Then he'll be whole in your tummy and it will be his own private burrow.'

Grace giggled uncertainly, but started chomping on his chocolate head. She offered me one arm because she felt he could manage on three paws. I'd imagined him so vividly I felt a little worried myself. It was like feasting on a real pet rabbit.

'You eat your rabbit all up yourself, Gracie,' I said.

'It's the loveliest treat ever,' she said indistinctly, mouth crammed with chocolate. 'But when did you buy it?' She paused. The obvious hit her. '*Where did you get the money?*'

'Keep your voice down!'

'I'm *whispering*.'

Then we heard the bedroom door open along the landing. We held our breath. I snapped the torch off and Grace leaped into her own bed. We

15

heard footsteps: the pad and slap of old slippers.

'It's OK, it's only Mum,' I whispered.

We heard her padding right along the landing, past our bedroom, down the stairs to the first floor, above the shop. Each stair creaked as she stepped. Our mother is a heavy woman.

We heard her in the kitchen, opening the fridge door.

'She's having a midnight feast too,' I muttered.

'Not a patch on mine,' Grace whispered, daring to take another bite.

Mum came trudging up the stairs again, slower now, breathing heavily.

'Should I save a little piece of rabbit for Mum?' Grace asked.

'No!'

'But she loves chocolate.'

'Ssh!'

'Not now. In the morning,' Grace persisted.

'Shut up or she'll hear us.'

It was too late. The footsteps stopped outside our door.

'Girls? Are you awake?' Mum whispered.

'No!' Grace said, idiotically.

Mum opened our door and came shuffling into the room. 'You should have gone to sleep ages ago,' she said. She came over to Grace's bed and bent over her. 'Are you all right, lovie?'

'Yes, Mum,' said Grace.

'What about you, Prudence?'

'I'm fine,' I mumbled, giving a little yawn to make her think I was on the brink of sleep.

16

'Are you hungry, Mum?' Grace asked. 'We heard you go down to the kitchen.'

'I was just getting a glass of milk for your dad. He's not feeling too clever. He keeps getting these funny turns.' Mum sounded very anxious.

'He should go to the doctor,' I said.

'You know what your dad's like,' said Mum. 'Prudence, why don't you try talking to him? When he's in a good mood? He might just listen to you.'

I pulled a face in the dark. I hated being Dad's favourite. It didn't really mean much anyway. I couldn't get him to do anything he didn't want to do. No one could.

'I'll try mentioning the doctor,' I said. 'But I don't think it will work.'

'You're a good girl,' said Mum. 'Well, night-night, then.'

She kissed Grace, patted my shoulder awkwardly and then waddled out of our bedroom, her hand held stiffly in front of her so she wouldn't spill the milk.

'You are a moron, Grace,' I hissed.

'Sorry!' she said. She took another big bite of chocolate bunny. 'Oh yum yum, happy tum!' She fell asleep in mid-munch, and started snoring softly.

I lay awake for a while, talking to Tobias.

2

I woke early and had another quick read of the teenage magazines before smoothing them out and hiding them under my mattress. I rescued the crackly cellophane from the bed and hid that too. It would be stupid to risk chucking it in the bin. In his maddest moments Dad would rootle right through the rubbish, mostly to berate Mum for buying the wrong things.

I went and got washed and then dressed in the red-and-white-check girly number. I plaited a strand of hair with scarlet thread and fastened it with three red beads. I wished I had red lipstick, but Dad wouldn't let us use make-up. It was a chilly morning so I stuck on my red cardigan too, an odd hand-knitted garment with a pixie hood.

Grace was still sound asleep, her lips crusted

with white chocolate. I hoped she'd have a good wash before she came downstairs for breakfast.

I heard snoring from Mum and Dad's bedroom so I thought I'd have the kitchen to myself. I made myself a cup of tea and then settled down at the kitchen table with my sketchpad and new watercolours, trying to reproduce the Tobias and the Angel painting from memory.

The back door suddenly opened, making me jump violently. My paintbrush blotched red paint, so that poor Tobias grew a massive muscly thigh.

'Good morning, Little Red Riding Hood,' said Dad, tweaking the limp woolly hood on my back.

I struggled into Winsome Daughter mode.

'Hi, Dad,' I said brightly, mopping at my painting with a hunched-up Kleenex. I was terrified that Dad would see my paintbox was new, bought with my stolen maths tuition money.

'Made a mistake?' said Dad, putting the kettle on to boil again.

'Well, you startled me a bit. I thought you were still asleep.' I closed the paintbox quickly, so that he wouldn't notice the paint palettes were pristine.

'I was just having a breath of fresh air in the garden.' Dad breathed in and out ostentatiously. 'Clearing the cobwebs.'

He swung his arms and beat his chest to indicate fitness. In actual fact he looked awful, very pale and drawn, his face so tense I could see the muscles jumping in his eyelid and temple.

He was wearing his old sleeveless padded jerkin. It had once been green but now it was a strange sludge colour. His shirtsleeves were rolled up very neatly in his usual painstaking way. His exposed arms were so thin that his long ropy veins looked about to burst through the skin.

'Are you all right, Dad?' I asked.

'Of course I am!' He glared at me indignantly. 'I'm in the pink.'

There was nothing remotely pink about his grey skin.

'What about these funny turns?' I said, chancing it.

It was a mistake.

'What's your mother been saying? There's nothing whatsoever wrong with me. Just because I had one little dizzy spell. She makes such a fuss.' Dad's eyes narrowed suspiciously. 'I suppose she's recruited you in her get-me-to-the-doctor campaign?'

'What?' I said, feigning ignorance. I tried hard to change the subject. 'What do you want for breakfast, Dad? Toast? A poached egg?'

'Not if *you're* poaching it, Prudence. It'll either be raw and runny or hard as a bullet,' said Dad, putting the poaching saucepan on the stove himself. 'You want to take some lessons from your mother.'

Dad had been a confirmed bachelor until Mum won him over with her Yorkshire puddings and treacle tarts. I knew she was an excellent cook but I didn't like that kind of old-fashioned

British food, all the pies and pastries and sauces and custards constructed from scratch. I hankered after convenience food and takeaways.

Grace and I knew every meal choice on the menu of the Kam Tong Chinese restaurant and the Ruby Curry House on our parade of shops but we'd never been allowed to eat there. We'd never even been able to order from Pete's Pizza takeaway round the corner, although Grace and I had spent ages choosing the perfect combination of toppings from the leaflet that came through the door. The only takeaway food we ever had was fish and chips once a month, and we'd even missed out on that recently because Dad had a bilious attack and blamed it on 'that greasy muck'.

I watched Dad fussing around with the poacher. He held an egg in either hand. 'You'll have one too, Prue?'

'No thanks, Dad.'

He tutted. 'You could do with the protein. You don't eat enough – unlike your tubby little sister.'

'Don't tell Grace she's tubby, Dad, she hates it,' I said.

'Don't *you* tell me how to talk to my own daughter, Miss Saucebox,' said Dad, poking me in the back. Then he patted my shoulder to show he was only joking. He leaned over, peering at my picture. 'That's not bad, girl,' he said.

'Not bad' is high praise from Dad. I couldn't help glowing.

'Our little trip to the National Gallery obviously inspired you,' Dad said proudly.

'It was wonderful. So, do you really think I'm good at art, Dad?'

'You know you are,' he said. 'In fact we *might* just collaborate when you're a wee bit older. You could design the dust wrapper for my Magnum Opus.'

Dad has been writing this so-called book ever since I was born. There are odd pages and half chapters all round the flat, typed on Dad's ancient Remington portable and scribbled over again and again with his cramped copperplate corrections. I've read pieces here and there and can't make sense of any of it. It's supposed to be a history of the world, but Dad seems mostly concerned with Kingtown, where we live, and how it's changed for the worse over the last thirty years.

Mum always arranges the discarded pages reverently, as if they're Ten Commandment tablets straight from God. She calls it Dad's Magnum Opus too, without a hint of irony. When Grace was a bit younger she thought Dad was writing about ice creams and showed a passing interest until I explained that Magnum Opus is Latin for 'great work'. Now we have a private running joke that Dad is writing an encyclopaedia of ice creams and we invent new extracts covering exotic flavours.

I decided I'd tell her Dad's idea and design a private dust wrapper for her amusement. Dad would be sitting in our bookshop with a Magnum in one hand, a Cornetto in the other, with Grace and me on either side of him carrying trays of ice-cream tubs for him to sample.

Dad saw me smiling and misunderstood. 'I'm not joking, Prudence. I really think you'd be good enough one day.'

I took a deep breath. Golden opportunity time!

'Maybe I'd need a little training, Dad,' I said casually, as if I didn't really care.

Dad raised his eyebrows and sighed. 'I'm not sending you to blooming art school,' he said. 'How many times do I have to get it into your thick head? Now don't go all droopy-drawers on me. You can paint as much as you like in your spare time. Anyway, they don't *paint* at art school now, they just faff around with blocks of concrete and dead animals and pretend all that crap is *creative*.'

I didn't bother replying. I stared at my painting of Tobias and the Angel. They smiled at me sympathetically with their rose-madder lips.

'If you've set your heart on further education, then you might as well go to a proper university,' said Dad. 'We'll show that interfering berk from the education authority. You'll pass all his exams with flying colours. How are you getting on with your maths tuition?'

I blinked. 'Fine, Dad,' I said quickly.

'I thought you said you couldn't understand a word she said?' Dad said suspiciously.

'And *you* said I just needed to apply myself – and I have,' I said. 'Dad, I'm sure your poached egg's ready. I'll make a pot of tea.'

I clattered around, and felt very relieved when Mum came thudding downstairs in her old pink mohair dressing gown. She's been wearing it ever since I can remember. It was a mistake right from the start. She looks like giant walking candyfloss.

'You two are early birds,' she said brightly. 'Oh, are you making breakfast, Prue? You're a good girl. Poached eggs – mm, lovely.'

'No, she's not making the poxy poached eggs; *I* am. And mine's ready now, but I suppose you want to nab it, so I'll just have to start all over again for mine,' said Dad.

'Oh no, dear, you have it. I'll make my own,' Mum twittered.

They started a totally pointless argument about eggs, while I packed up my painting and made tea and toast for four, thankful that I'd somehow managed to skirt round the maths tuition inquisition.

I relaxed too soon. We were still sitting at the breakfast table fifteen minutes later, Mum fussing, Dad irritated, Grace in her teddy pyjamas sleepily scoffing half a packet of cornflakes, when we heard the post come through the shop letter box.

'More blooming bills,' said Dad. 'Run and fetch them, Prudence.'

I ran. I fetched. I didn't even think to sort

through the little wad of envelopes. I saw there was one white handwritten envelope but I didn't wonder who it could be from.

I'd written a very good showy essay for Dad on the significance of letters in Victorian fiction – and yet I was thick enough to hand it straight to him. Dad shuffled the envelopes, opening them with his eggy knife, chucking several bills straight into the bin.

'We can't just ignore them, Bernard,' Mum said anxiously.

'Yes we can,' said Dad.

'But we're going to have to pay *some*time.'

'I don't know what with,' said Dad, flapping another sheet of paper at her. 'This is from the bank. "Overdraft . . . not acceptable . . . blah-di-blah." Jumped up little penpusher. I don't need *him* to point out my financial circumstances, thanks very much.'

That letter went in the bin too. Mum twitched, peering over at it, ready to whisk it out the minute Dad left the room.

He binned the next letter too, barely reading it.

'What was that about, dear?' Mum asked anxiously.

'That interfering creep Miles from the education authority. He's still banging on about Prudence's GCSE coaching. Demanding details, tutors' names, timetables! God almighty!'

'Well, that's OK, dear. We've got Prue started at Miss Roberts's. Then maybe we can manage

25

some science tuition later on. But you'd better write and let him know. Just in case he might turn nasty.'

'Let him try! Now, what's this?' said Dad. He slit open the white envelope, took out the sheet of paper and read the letter. He sat very still.

'Prudence?' he said quietly.

My heart started thudding under my red-and-white checks. 'Yes?'

'This is a letter from Miss Roberts,' Dad said ominously.

I swallowed. Grace nudged up close to me.

'Oh dear,' said Mum. 'Doesn't she think Prue's been making any progress?'

'Well. You could say that,' said Dad, spinning it out. His whole body was tensed, ready to spring.

'Now don't go getting cross with her, Bernard. It's not her fault she finds maths a puzzle. I'm sure she's doing her best,' said Mum.

'Yes, she's doing her best, all right,' said Dad, his voice rising. His pale face flushed purple. 'Doing her best to make a monkey out of me!'

He shouted it, spit spraying into the air. Then he wavered, wobbling sideways so that he had to clutch the table.

'Don't get so het up, please,' Mum begged. 'Are you having another funny turn?'

'Yes, I am – and it's no blooming wonder!' Dad said, through clenched teeth. He leaned over the table at me. 'How *dare* you!' he yelled, thumping the old scratched pine so hard that all the plates and knives and spoons rattled.

Grace reached out and held my hand under the table.

'What has she *done*, Bernard?' Mum asked. 'Has this Miss Roberts complained about her? Maybe she's simply too strict for our Prue.'

'Miss Roberts hasn't complained, as such. She's simply a little perturbed. She hasn't seen hide nor hair of Prudence for the last three weeks.'

'What?' said Mum. 'But – but why? Did you get lost, Prue? Why didn't you go?'

'Well?' Dad shouted, leaning so far over the table his face was nearly touching mine.

'I went once and I couldn't understand a thing. I just didn't see the point,' I muttered.

'I can't believe I'm hearing this!' Dad bellowed. 'Why didn't you come and tell me, after your one obviously disastrous visit?'

'I didn't want to,' I said, right into his face.

'You didn't want to. Even though you knew Mr Miles is all set to leap into action and slam your mother and me behind bars for not giving you a proper education?'

'He won't put us in prison! Will he?' Mum said weakly.

'Of course you won't go to prison, Mum.'

'Oh, Miss Know-It-All! Only you know damn all, even though you think you're so smart. You need to get to grips with maths, even if you're just going to waste your time at art college. Remember that, missy. You thought you could swan off and do your own thing, tell bare-faced

27

lies to your own father, waste everyone's time and money—'

He stopped short, his mouth still working silently though he'd run out of words.

'Bernard? Do calm down – you're getting yourself in such a state. You're making yourself ill!' said Mum, catching hold of his arm.

He brushed her away as if she was some irritating insect. He focused on me. His face was still purple. Even his eyes were bloodshot with his rage. 'What about my money?' he screamed. 'What have you done with my eighty pounds?'

'Sixty. I paid the first time.'

'Don't you dare quibble with me! Sixty, eighty, whatever. Hand it over immediately, do you hear me?'

'I can't.'

Dad struggled to draw breath. He looked as if his head was about to explode, shooting eyes, teeth, tongue all over the table. 'I said *hand it over immediately*!'

'I can't, Dad. I've spent it,' I said.

Dad reeled. 'You've spent eighty pounds of my money?' he gasped.

'Sixty pounds, Dad. Yes. I'm sorry,' I said weakly.

'Whatever did you spend it on, Prudence?' Mum whispered.

I swallowed, unable to say.

'She spent it on me. On chocolate. Lots and lots and lots of chocolate,' Grace gabbled desperately.

28

'I might have known. You greedy little fool!' said Dad in disgust. 'So you stuffed your great gut with *my* hard-earned money.'

I was suddenly so angry I wasn't frightened of Dad any more.

'Don't talk to Grace like that, Dad. It's horrible, and it's so unfair. I *didn't* spend the money on chocolate. Grace is just saying that to protect me. I spent it on other stuff.'

'*What* stuff?' said Mum, who'd never spent sixty pounds in one go in her life.

'I went to McDonald's, I bought magazines, I got a special box of watercolours from the art shop—'

'That wouldn't use up eighty whole pounds! Give me what's left!'

'Sixty, Dad, *sixty*! I spent all of it. I bought some underwear too.'

'Underwear?' Dad gasped. 'What sort of an idiot do you take me for, Prudence? What did you really buy?'

'Oh my lord, you're not on drugs, are you?' said Mum.

I'd never had the chance to smoke so much as a Silk Cut, never swallowed anything more sinister than an aspirin. The idea that I'd somehow been hobnobbing with drug dealers was so ludicrous I couldn't help smiling.

Dad's hand shot out. I felt such a whack on my cheek that I nearly toppled sideways.

'Take that smirk off your face! Now tell me what you spent eighty pounds on, you little liar.'

Grace started crying, but I was too angry for tears.

'It was *sixty* pounds, Dad – don't you ever listen? And I *told* you, I bought my watercolour paints, some food in McDonald's, some magazines . . . and some underwear.'

'Show me!' said Dad.

'Don't, Bernard! Of course she can't show you,' Mum said. She looked at me worriedly, putting her hand on my scarlet cheek. She rubbed at it, as if she could wipe the slap away.

'I'll show him,' I said. 'I'll go and get it.'

'No – don't, Prue!' Grace wept. 'She really did buy me chocolate, Dad, a great big bunny, I swear she did.'

'Ssh, Grace. Dad won't believe you. He thinks we're both liars. Well, we'll show him.'

I strode to the bedroom, pulled open my drawer, found my beautiful new bra and knickers, took hold of them in each hand, ran back and threw them down on the table in front of Dad.

He recoiled as if they were hissing vipers. We all stared at the pink satin bra, the padded cups standing out proudly, edged with black lace. The wispy matching knickers curled in an S shape, barely wider than a ribbon.

Behind the table the family's damp underwear hung limply on the airer, grey-white, baggy, slackly elasticated, almost interchangeable.

'You sleazy disgusting little trollop!' Dad shouted. 'You're no daughter of mine.'

'I don't *want* to be your daughter. You're the worst father in the whole world!' I shouted back.

He clutched his chest as if I'd punched him. Then he fell forward, his head going smack against our old table. I thought he was literally banging his head with rage. I waited for him to sit up again.

Dad stayed where he was.

'Oh Bernard!' Mum whispered.

'Dad?' said Grace.

The kitchen was suddenly appallingly silent. I stared across the table.

I had killed my own father.

We stayed sitting still for a second, staring at Dad. It was Grace who suddenly sprang into action, surprising all of us.

'We should bang his chest and give him the kiss of life!' she said, running round the table towards Dad.

She took hold of him fearfully, pulling him backwards into an upright position. Very bravely, she tilted his head, took a deep breath and blew into his mouth in a ghastly parody of a kiss.

We had never kissed Dad on his mouth in our lives.

Seeing my poor sister behaving so valiantly jerked me into action too.

'An ambulance! I'll dial nine nine nine,' I said.

'No, no, your dad won't go to hospital,' Mum wept, though Dad was clearly past arguing.

I dialled anyway. Someone at the end of the line asked me which service I wanted. I asked for an ambulance and gave our address.

'I should have asked for the police too,' I said. 'So they could come and arrest me.'

'Don't be so silly,' said Mum, rushing round, starting to clear the table. Her hand hovered over my pink and black lace underwear. 'Take these, Prue, quick!'

I stuffed them in the pocket of my frock and went and stood beside Grace. I watched her labouring over Dad.

'You're doing it too quickly. And shouldn't you pinch his nostrils?'

'*You* do it, Prue,' said Mum.

I had a go, although it was awful shoving my head so close to Dad, feeling his coarse moustache scratching my lips, his false teeth clunking against mine. I scooped them out, feeling I was violating my own father.

Mum tried too, though she seemed as reluctant as me. She kept stopping and peering at him fearfully, as if he was about to strike her for being so impertinent.

My cheek still throbbed from his slap. I started pacing up and down, peering out of the window for the ambulance, as if I could summon it up instantly by willpower.

'Get . . . Dad's . . . pyjamas,' Mum gasped, in between breaths.

'I'll pack a case for him, Mum,' Grace said quickly.

It seemed bizarre, finding nightclothes and a toothbrush and a flannel for someone who might already be dead. He still wasn't moving at all, and his eyes were semi-shut. Mum hovered above him, bent over awkwardly, her head on his chest. I thought she might be hugging him, but she was listening for a heartbeat.

'I think I can hear it. You listen, Prue. It *is* his heart, isn't it?'

I couldn't tell if the drumming in my ear was my own blood or his. I hated breathing in Dad's stale old-book, old-sweat, old-jersey smell. His mouth was lopsided now, as if he was silently groaning. He looked like an old, old man.

'Oh Dad,' I said, and I started crying. 'I didn't mean to make you so angry. I'm sorry. Can you hear me? I'm so so sorry.'

There was a knock on the shop door downstairs. The ambulance people were here. They gently prised me off Dad and examined him carefully.

'Is he dead?' I sobbed.

'No, no! He's unconscious, dear, but he's not dead. We'll get him to hospital as soon as possible.'

'He hates hospitals,' said Mum.

'Can't help that, love. We can't leave him here in this state. Are you coming with him?'

'Yes, of course, he's my husband.'

'What about the girls? They'd best stay here.'

Mum looked at us, biting her lip.

'Do you want me to come, Mum?' I said.

34

Mum drew in her breath, hugging her huge chest, her hands hanging onto her elbows. 'No, dear, you stay and look after Grace. I'll ring you from the hospital. You be good girls and – and try not to worry.'

The ambulance people strapped Dad onto a stretcher and manoeuvred him out of the kitchen and down the stairs, Mum treading heavily behind with the carrier of his things. Grace and I followed them downstairs and through the shop, as if we were in some strange procession. We watched from the shop doorway as they slotted Dad's stretcher into the ambulance and helped Mum clamber inside too.

The Chinese people stood on their restaurant doorstep, watching. They nodded at us sympathetically. 'Your dad?' they said, and the woman pointed to her heart.

When the ambulance drove off she asked us if we'd like to come and sit with them.

'No, no, it's very kind, but we're fine,' I said firmly.

Grace pushed me when we were back inside our own shop. 'I wanted to see what their place is like. And they might have given us some chow mein and chop suey – I *so* want to know what it tastes like.' Then she clapped her hands over her mouth. 'I didn't mean that. Dad's right, I *am* a greedy guts. Oh Prue, this is all so awful. I can't believe it, can you?'

'Remember when we were little and Dad sent

us to bed in disgrace and then we'd curl up and pretend to be different people?'

'Yeah, I liked it best when I was Kylie Little Bum and you were Janet Air and I sang and you painted and we lived in our own penthouse flat,' said Grace, sighing. 'You're always so good at making everything up.'

'Maybe it isn't good. It takes over from your real life and you start to believe it. Like when I bought the knickers and bra. I was pretending to be like the girls in the magazines and then when I argued with Dad I was kidding myself I was like little Jane Eyre standing up to Mr Brocklehurst – and yet look what I've done.'

'He'll get better, Prue. The ambulance people said he was just unconscious. So maybe he just fainted because he was so mad at you?'

'Don't be daft, Grace. He wasn't just *fainting*,' I said.

'Well. Whatever. But it wasn't *your* fault. You didn't make him ill.'

'I did, I did. I don't know how I could have yelled back at him like that.'

'I thought you were brave. I'd never dare. But I get on Dad's nerves more than you do. It's because I'm so fat and so stupid. No wonder he likes you best,' Grace said, with no hint of resentment.

'I think Dad's the stupid one. You're much much much nicer than me. You'd definitely be *my* favourite, Gracie,' I said, and I put my arms round her.

We had a long hug and then broke away, looking at each other anxiously. The kitchen seemed spookily quiet in spite of the loud hum of our old fridge and the tick of the clock. We both watched the second hand edging its way round each numeral.

We'd rarely been in the house by ourselves. We'd frequently fantasized about days of freedom together but now we were too frightened and guilty to do anything but stand and stare.

'When do you think Mum will come back?' said Grace. She swallowed. 'I mean, I know you don't know either, but do you think she'll be back by lunch time? And what should we do about the shop? Will we open it up?'

'There's not much point. How many customers do we get?' I said.

I went to the waste bin and fished out all the bills. 'Look, final demand, final demand. And – oh God, look at this one – they're threatening to take Dad to court, Grace. I think he's going to have to close the shop anyway, even if he gets better.'

'But what will he do? Do you think he'll publish his Magnum Whatsit?'

'Oh, come on, Grace, he's never going to finish it.'

I thought of Dad only an hour ago, admiring my Tobias and the Angel painting and telling me I could illustrate his precious book. I started howling.

'Oh don't, Prue! Dad will be all right, I'm sure he will be,' Grace said, clutching me.

'I was so *mean* to him. I let him down so. And if we're really in all this debt it's so awful that I spent all his tuition money. No wonder he was so cross. How must he have felt when I thrust my bra and knickers right in his face?' I pulled them out of my pocket and tugged hard at them, but they wouldn't rip. I rummaged in the kitchen cupboard for the scissors.

'No! Don't! *I'll* have them if you don't want them,' Grace said quickly.

I stared at her.

'I know they wouldn't fit me, but I could just keep them like – like secret ornaments,' she said. 'They are *so* beautiful. Where did you get them from?'

'Mallard and Turners. Their underwear department.'

'You went there by yourself? You lucky thing!'

We looked at each other. We had the perfect opportunity to slip out now and go round all the forbidden shops, but of course we couldn't.

'We can't go on a jaunt, not while Dad's so ill or—'

'I know,' said Grace, sighing. 'So what *shall* we do?'

'Perhaps we ought to get on with our work, same as any other day. That's kind of pleasing Dad, isn't it?'

So we cleared the kitchen table and got out our books and notebooks and pens. Grace tried

to do a passage of English comprehension. I
tried to read a chapter of a French children's
book.

We sighed and stared into space a lot, unable
to concentrate. I made myself a cup of black
coffee to see if that would jerk me into
attentiveness. Grace got the cereal packet and
the sugar bowl and dipped and nibbled between
sentences.

I threw my French book across the room after
an hour and got out my paints and my Tobias
and the Angel picture, deciding to finish it. I
tried talking to Tobias in my head but Grace
kept interrupting.

'Can I use your paints too?' she begged. 'I want
to make Dad a Get Well Soon card.'

I was scared it was a bit late in the day for
a Get Well Soon card but I didn't dare say it. I
hated Grace using my paints because she
always put too much water on her brush and
turned the neat little palettes into muddy pools,
but I decided I'd better be kind to her.

She laboured long and hard over her card.
She used the back of the cornflake packet so
that it would stand up stiffly. She drew our
bookshop, dutifully painting each individual
book red or green or brown or blue, although
they merged into each other as one long book
blob. Then she drew Dad, a little skinny man
with a frowny face. She drew Mum, a big blobby
woman with black dots for eyes and similar dots
all over her dress. All the dots ran so that it

looked as if Mum and her dress were weeping copiously. She drew me in a corner, reading a book, my hair very thick and bushy so my face seemed hidden by a black cloud. She drew herself wearing her favourite pink panda dress, like a big raspberry meringue.

'Have you finished? That's so good,' I said.

'It's not. I'm rubbish at painting. I could see the way I wanted it to be in my head but it won't come out right on the paper,' Grace sighed. She looked at it worriedly. 'I've made Dad too small.'

'He *is* small. Smaller than Mum.'

'He looks like a stick, like he'll snap any minute,' Grace wailed. 'Help me make him look bigger, Prue.'

'He's fine,' I said, but I stopped applying delicate touches of gold ink to the Angel's halo and helped her lengthen Dad's arms and legs.

'He still doesn't look right. He's like one of those insect thingies with long legs,' said Grace.

'Daddy-longlegs,' I said.

We laughed though it wasn't a bit funny. Grace looked as if she might cry again any minute.

'I wish Mum would come back,' she said. 'Is it lunch time yet?'

It was only just gone eleven but I made her French toast to cheer her up. We had another round each at half past twelve, and finished all the flapjacks in the tin, and ate an overripe banana mid-afternoon.

Mum didn't get back till five. Her eyes were red, and she was clutching a sodden handkerchief.

'He's dead!' I whispered.

I started sobbing. So did Grace.

'No, no, he's not dead. There, girls. I'm so sorry – you must have been very worried. I was in such a state I forgot to check I had any change for the phone call. I had no idea they would take so long. It's a nightmare, a total nightmare. Your dad's going to be so angry with me when he realizes he's in hospital. Well, maybe he *does* know. It's hard to tell.' Mum started crying too.

'Is he still unconscious then, Mum?'

'Well, his eyes are open and maybe he understands. But he can't speak, you see.'

'What do you mean? Has he done something to his throat?'

'No, no. Your father's suffered a stroke, girls. It's affected his speech and he can't use his arm and his leg.'

'But he'll get better, won't he, Mum?' said Grace.

'They don't know, darling. It's too early to tell at this stage.'

I went running out of the room. I threw myself on my bed. I couldn't bear it. I knew it was all my fault.

A stroke is such a strangely inappropriate term to describe what's happened to Dad. The word 'stroke' implies something soft and subtle. Dad looks as if he's been bashed repeatedly down one side. His head lolls, his mouth droops, and his right arm and leg sag as if they're broken.

Mum had warned us but it was still terrifying walking along the ward of the stroke unit and going into Dad's room. The man slumped in the bed was a Guy Fawkes caricature of our father.

We stood on the threshold of his room, all three of us. Dad's eyes were closed, but he mumbled something.

'Hello, Dad,' I whispered, forcing myself to walk over to his bed.

His eyes snapped open, making me jump. He frowned at me. There was a little dribble down his chin. He tried to wipe it away, looking agonized.

'Shall I wipe it, Dad?' I asked.

He made vehement mumbles, making it plain he didn't want to be helped at all. He carried on struggling after his chin was dry. He kept flinging his unaffected leg out from under the bedclothes, hoping that the rest of his body would follow.

'Lie still, dear. Try to relax,' said Mum.

Dad's contorted face was anything but relaxed. He tried again and again.

'He's trying to get out of bed to go home,' I said.

Dad glared at me, groaning. He resented me talking about him rather than to him.

I went closer, though I really wanted to run away, out of the room, down the ward, right out of the hospital.

'Dad, you can't go home just yet, you're not well enough,' I said.

Dad wouldn't see reason. He became more and more agitated, and when Mum tried to tuck him back under the sheets he punched her arm. It was the weakest, feeblest punch in the world, but it made her cry.

'Now, now, there's no need for tears,' said a nurse, bustling in and putting her arm round Mum. She was nearly as large as Mum, but in an exuberant, voluptuous way. She had glossy brown skin and magnificent plaited hair. 'Mr King's doing splendidly, my dear. Aren't you, lovie?'

She nodded at Dad and then stuck a thermometer in his mouth before he could groan at her. He spat it straight out defiantly.

'You're a naughty boy,' she said, laughing. 'You want to have a little game with me? Watch out, though, laddie – I might well stick it somewhere else if you turn awkward on me.'

Dad decided to subject himself to a thermometer in his mouth after all.

'There now. That's the ticket.' The nurse winked at Mum. 'We'll soon get him trained, eh?'

Mum simpered uneasily. 'He hates hospitals so,' she said.

'Well, we're none of us here by choice,' said the nurse. 'I'd much sooner be at home with my feet up watching *Corrie* on the telly.'

Dad groaned again, gargling slightly with the thermometer.

'Hey, hey, watch out or you'll swallow it,' said the nurse. 'OK, let's see how you're doing.'

'How's his temperature?' Mum asked anxiously.

'It's fine, dear, just fine. You're doing well, Mr King,' the nurse said. 'Let's just tidy you up a bit in honour of your visitors.' She smoothed his pyjama collar and combed his sparse hair with her long brown fingers. He did his best to bat her away, groaning something that sounded very much like a bad swearword.

The nurse seemed to think it was too. 'Ooh! In front of your wife and daughters! I'll wash your mouth out with soap if you're not careful,'

44

she said cheerily. She raised her eyebrows at Mum, and then shook her head. Mum shook her head back, though she glanced anxiously at Dad.

The nurse smiled at me. 'So what's your name, dear? I'm Nurse Ray. Little ray of sunshine, that's me.'

'I'm Prudence,' I said, wincing, because I hate my name so much.

'And what about you, sweetheart?' said Nurse Ray, going over to Grace. She'd been skulking fearfully in a corner the whole time.

'I'm Grace,' she whispered.

Dad groaned as if the very sound of her name irritated him.

'Don't look so worried, sweetheart,' said Nurse Ray, chucking Grace under the chin. 'Daddy's only grumpy because he's had his stroke. He'll be his usual self in no time, I'm sure.'

Grace stared at her. Dad was very much his usual self, even incapacitated by his stroke. He didn't *have* any other self. He was permanently grumpy.

'Go and say hello to your dad. It'll cheer him up,' said Nurse Ray.

She encouraged Grace forwards until she was in Dad's line of sight. He saw her approaching. He groaned again.

'Hello, Dad. I've made you a Get Well Soon card,' Grace said bravely.

Dad made little attempt to look at it.

'Hold it up above Daddy's head so he can see it properly,' said Nurse Ray.

45

Grace waved her card around in the air above Dad. He moaned, his eyes swivelling, as if a vulture was circling above him. He made another attempt to get his leg out of bed. He heaved himself halfway up with his good arm, beads of sweat standing out on his forehead.

'Oh Bernard, don't, dear, you'll hurt yourself,' Mum flapped, patting at him.

'I'm sorry, Mr King, you're stuck with us for a while,' said Nurse Ray, expertly flipping him down on his back and tucking him in firmly. 'It's not going to be for too long. Believe me, we need the beds. We just need you to be a bit stronger and start getting more vocal and mobile. That makes sense, doesn't it?'

Dad groaned feebly, but lay still and shut his eyes.

'That's it. You have a little nap.'

We said goodnight to him and backed out of the room. Nurse Ray came with us, smiling encouragement.

'How long will my husband have to stay in hospital?' Mum asked.

'It's up to the doctors, dear. It'll depend on what sort of progress your husband makes.'

'Will he get better?' I asked. 'Properly better?'

Nurse Ray hesitated. 'He'll get a lot better, I'm sure.'

'Will he be able to talk again? And walk?'

'I dare say. Some people make complete recoveries.'

'But some don't?'

'Your daddy's a fighter, cussed as they come. His type generally do the best.' She seemed keen to change the subject, concentrating on my hideous red-checked dress. 'Is that your school uniform?' she said sympathetically.

'I don't go to school,' I said, blushing.

'They're home-educated,' said Mum. 'My husband teaches them.' She stopped short and put her hand to her mouth. She didn't say any more.

I wondered what on earth was going to happen now.

Mum made us beans on toast when we got home, which was quick and comforting. We listened to the radio while we ate, and then started sewing our quilt. I'd designed the overall pattern and cut out all the little hexagons, Grace tacked as best she could, and Mum sewed. It was so peaceful listening to quiz shows on Radio Four without Dad's incessant interruptions: *'Don't you know that, you fool?' 'Come on, come on, speak up!' 'Fatuous idiot, who does he think he is?'* He addressed the radio speaker, as if all the performers were actually inside, little tiny men, listening.

We knew we had to talk about Dad and what was going to happen, but none of us could bear to spoil the peace. Grace and I went up to bed at our usual time. I was in the middle of reading a biography of Queen Elizabeth I for my Tudor project but I didn't feel like history.

I knelt down by my bookcase and fingered my

way through all my favourite old books. I found my big battered nursery rhyme book wedged right at the back, with weirdly worrying pictures of jumping cows and blind mice and girls with giant spiders. I flicked through this surreal world where pigs went marketing and children lived in shoes and the moon was made of green cheese.

I remembered Dad's pedantic voice enunciating, 'Ring-a-ring-a-roses' and 'Hey diddle diddle'. I'd never been invited to sit on Dad's lap when he read to me, but I'd sit cross-legged at his feet.

'Do you remember Dad reading us nursery rhymes?' I asked Grace.

'I didn't like them because they were scary. He poked me hard and told me not to be so soft,' said Grace.

I hesitated. 'Grace, do you love Dad?'

'Of course I do!' Grace said.

'But sometimes don't you hate him too?'

'Never,' said Grace, sounding shocked.

'Not even when he's being particularly horrid? He's much meaner to you than he is to me.'

'Yes, but that's because I'm thick.'

'No you're *not*! Listen, *I* hate him.'

'You can't say that, Prue, not now he's ill.'

'But it doesn't make him any nicer, does it? Weren't you embarrassed, him going on like that in front of that nurse?'

'She was so lovely,' said Grace. 'That's what I'd like to be now, a nurse. I could look after people and make them better and have them think me special. If I can't pass exams to get to

48

be a proper nurse maybe I could go in one of those big homes and look after old folk.'

'Are you going to help nurse Dad then?'

'Oh! No, I couldn't! I mean, he wouldn't let me.'

'So who *is* going to nurse him?' I said.

I felt terrified. What if it had to be *me*?

I stayed awake hours after Grace nodded off. I heard Mum go to bed, but when I got up to go to the loo her light was still on. I put my head round the door. She was still wearing her pink dressing gown, sitting on the end of the bed, staring into space.

'Mum?'

'Oh Prue!' She had tears trickling down her face.

'Don't cry, Mum.' I went to sit beside her, reaching up and putting my arm right round her large shoulders. 'Maybe Dad will make a complete recovery, like that nurse said.'

'Maybe,' said Mum, but we neither of us believed it. 'I'm just trying to figure out what to do. I don't know what's the matter with me. I don't know if it's living with your dad all these years. He's always told me what to do, and now it's as if my mind won't work. Not that it ever did very much. I was never a thinker, not like you and your dad. I was always in awe of your dad whenever he came in to buy his pie and his sausage roll from the baker's where I worked – you know, where the Chinese folk are now. He knew so much, and he had all his books. He lived in a different world.'

'Well, he obviously fancied the pretty young girl in the baker's or he would never have asked you out,' I said, patting her.

'I wasn't ever pretty, dear. And it wasn't your dad made the first move, it was me. I got up the courage to ask if he'd like me to do any dusting or tidying in the shop. Then I cooked him a meal. That's how it all started.'

'And you've been dusting and tidying and cooking ever since,' I said. 'It's going to be all right, Mum. We'll sort things out together.'

'I don't know where to start. I don't know how I'm going to cope when your dad comes out of hospital.'

'I'll help, Mum.' I took a deep breath. 'I suppose I can take a turn if Dad needs any nursing.' My chest was so tight I could hardly get the words out. Mum shook her head.

'No,' she said firmly. 'That's one thing I do know. You're still only a child, even though you're so clever. I'm not having you take on such a burden. Anyway, you won't be around during the day. You'll be at school.'

I stared at her.

'You'll have to start school, Prue – you and Grace. Your dad won't be in a fit state to teach you, and I certainly can't. There's so much you need to know for these exams. We can't send you for tuition in all the different subjects, we simply can't afford it.'

'I'm so sorry about taking Miss Roberts's money, Mum.'

'Oh well. It's not as if you've made a habit of it. I've felt badly for years that you girls have so little spending money – though I wish you'd spent it on something *sensible*, rather than those lacy little bits of nothing.'

'I know. It's just . . . I so wanted them.'

'Yes, of course you did. Don't you think *I* ever want things?' Mum saw me staring and burst out laughing. '*Not* fancy underwear. Those knicks of yours wouldn't even go round my knee as a garter. No, there's all sorts of things I'd love. Not clothes, I'm not worth dressing.' Mum slapped at her thighs contemptuously, as if they were two great stupid beasts beyond her control. 'But I'd love stuff for the house, all the labour-saving gadgets, and oh goodness, how I'd love a television just like anyone else. I've tried to get your dad to see it's educational but he won't hear of it. He's just books books books. Still, even he can see you can't learn *everything* from books. You need to go to school so you can start studying for your GCSEs. Grace can start too – she needs the extra pushing.'

I'd been begging Dad to send me to school for years and years. I'd read every school book avidly. I'd skied through all the Chalet School books, I'd sniggered at Angela Brazil's *Bosom Friends*, I'd attended St Clare's with the twins, I'd been to Hogwarts with Harry. But these were old-fashioned schools, figments of the imagination.

I thought about Wentworth High School, the grim concrete building three roads away, on the edge of the Wentworth Estate. I'd no idea what it was like inside. You couldn't even peer into the playground, because there was a high creosoted fence, with barbed wire scalloping the top in sinister fashion. I didn't know if it was to stop intruders or imprison the pupils.

I imagined myself walking into that bleak building.

'It won't be Wentworth High, will it?' I said.

Boys from Wentworth sometimes came banging and shouting into the shop, throwing books around, asking if Dad stocked crazy rude titles. He'd order them out of the shop and threaten to call the police. He tried phoning the school to complain, but he said the teachers sounded as uncouth as the pupils.

'Your dad would die if you went to Wentworth,' said Mum. Then she clapped her hand over her mouth. 'No, no,' she said indistinctly. 'We'll send you to Kingtown High. Your dad went there, when it was a grammar school. He'd like to think you were following in his footsteps. Though maybe he'd feel happier if it was an all girls' school. That's it, we'll find you a nice decent girls' school.'

She said it as if she could conjure up a demure convent directly down the road. I saw myself in a straw boater and blazer, arm in arm with my best friend Jane. We'd giggle together and share secrets. It wouldn't matter if we were the odd ones out, because we'd have each other.

I pictured Grace tagging along behind us on

our way to school. I felt sorry for her, so I gave her a best friend too, a roly-poly red-cheeked little girl who loved Grace dearly and stuck up for her whenever she was teased. I even imagined Mum making friends with some of the other mums while Dad nodded benignly in the background, a gentle, frail invalid . . .

We had to go to Wentworth. All the other schools were full up, with long waiting lists.

'We can't go to Wentworth, Mum!' I said. 'We won't go. You need me to help out in the shop now, anyway.'

'We can't risk it. If that education inspector chappie comes back and catches you working then we'll really be prosecuted,' said Mum. 'No, Prue, you're starting at Wentworth next Monday, it's all fixed.'

'But Mum, I don't *want* to go to Wentworth. Look, you *said*—'

'I know what I said. But I can't help it. I don't know what else I can do. For God's sake, can't you try to make this easier for me? Don't you see I'm at the end of my tether?'

I wasn't sure what a tether was. I imagined

a long fraying rope with Mum tied on the end, fat legs dangling.

'OK, OK. Don't you worry, Mum, we'll go,' I said.

'But it'll be *awful*,' Grace wept in our bedroom that night. 'When I go to the sweet shop these girls from Wentworth are always making faces at me and whispering and giggling. I know they're talking about me. And they steal stuff, I've seen them. And the boys are worse, you know they are.'

'Don't go *on* about it, Grace,' I said, because I wanted to drift off with Tobias into our own private world.

'It's all right for you. You're pretty and skinny and clever. You'll make heaps of friends. But what about me? They'll all pick on me and tease me because I'm fat.'

'No they won't. Well, if they do, I'll bash them up,' I said fiercely, though I wasn't sure I could bash so much as a boiled egg.

Grace looked a bit doubtful too.

'Look, if it's really really awful we simply won't go,' I said. 'We'll pretend we're going, but we'll just hang out round the town, go for walks, whatever, just like I did when I was supposed to be seeing that awful Miss Roberts.'

'Really?' said Grace. She sat up in bed and blew her nose. 'Oh Prue, don't let's go at all. Let's just bunk off right from the start. It will be fun!'

'Well, you'll have to keep it absolutely quiet. No blurting it out to Mum!'

'I'll keep my lips totally sealed, I promise,' Grace said.

Mum started fussing on Sunday night about what we were to wear.

'I phoned up on Friday and explained it might be a problem getting both of you kitted out for uniform. I hoped I'd find something in BHS but no one does that green, and even so, the prices are ludicrous. They told me there's a second-hand school uniform shop open every Friday. It's meant to be very reasonable, so you'll be able to get yourselves sorted out. Meanwhile you'll just have to wear your dresses and cardies and explain if anyone asks.'

'Yes, Mum,' we said meekly.

'You've to be at school at quarter to nine tomorrow, to see the headteacher. I expect she's going to give you a little pep talk. There's no need to be nervous. Don't worry, I'll come too.'

We blinked at her.

Mum smoothed down her skirt and then looked at it properly. It wasn't really a proper skirt at all; it was a length of chintz curtain material Mum had hastily stitched together in a depressing dirndl shape. She'd put on even more weight meanwhile. She stared at the big red roses stretched to the limit around her vast thighs.

'Oh dear,' she said. 'I wonder if my good suit still fits.'

'You don't have to come to Wentworth with us, Mum,' I said quickly.

'Of course I do,' said Mum. 'Your dad can't go, obviously, so it's down to me.'

'*No*, Mum. We'll look stupid, going with you,' I said.

Mum looked at me, her face flushing as red as her roses.

'Look, I didn't mean because you're *you*,' I said hurriedly. 'We just don't want to walk in with our *mum*. The other kids will laugh at us.'

'Then they'll have to laugh,' said Mum, her chin up. 'I'm coming, Prudence. I need to be there. I've got to make sure you *go* there for a start.' She looked me straight in the eye. It was my turn to blush.

'Oh Mum, we don't want to go,' Grace wailed, and started howling.

Mum sat down on the sofa and pulled Grace onto her lap. 'There now, baby,' she said, rocking her.

'Everything's so horrible and scary and different,' Grace wept.

'I know, I know,' said Mum, rubbing her cheek across the top of Grace's mousy hair. 'I don't want you to go to school, poppet. Heaven knows, I hated it myself. But now your dad's not able to teach you we'll just have to give it a go. And maybe . . . maybe it's time you two learned to fit in more. I just want you both to be happy.'

We looked the picture of misery the next morning, walking to Wentworth in our ridiculous home-made clothes. Mum's suit wouldn't fit her so she was squeezed back into the red rose number, with a red knitted jumper rammed down over her big bosom. Grace was wearing her pink pandas. I told her it maybe *did* look babyish, which hurt her feelings, but she insisted on wearing it because it was her favourite frock.

I cordially hated *all* my frocks, but chose the red and white check as the least offensive. I wore my new black and pink lace underwear underneath, for courage. I hoped it might make me feel like one of the Wentworth girls, confident and sexy and streetwise.

As soon as we set foot inside the great gates everyone stared at us. We trekked across the playground. It seemed as large as the Sahara Desert. I realized that two little strips of hidden lace weren't going to make the slightest difference. Some of the kids had big grins on their faces. It was as if a circus had stopped at their school. We were the clowns.

The girls stood in little groups, giggling. The boys started jostling each other and shouting. Mum looked at Grace and me anxiously and then reached out to hold our hands. She was trying to reassure us but this was a *big* mistake. I snatched my hand away immediately but Grace clung to Mum. That made their jeers increase.

'Let go!' I hissed.

They took no notice, clutching each other. I sighed and marched ahead. I kept my head up and didn't look round, no matter what they shouted. Now I'd jettisoned Mum and Grace I imagined Jane on one side of me, Tobias the other. We didn't care what they called. We were a threesome, cool, aloof, artistic . . .

'God, what do they *look* like? Mum's a walking sofa, the little blobby one's a duvet and the skinny stuck-up cow's a tablecloth!' someone yelled.

I couldn't stay cool. I felt tears pricking my eyes. I turned round and stuck my finger up at them. They all shrieked delightedly. Mum looked shocked.

'Prudence! Don't do that.'

'What did she do, Mum? Prue, what does it mean, doing that with your finger?' said Grace.

'I don't know,' I lied. I'd seen the boys from the estate gesture to each other and worked out exactly what it meant. Grace didn't seem to have any idea at all. She was looking younger than ever, and very frightened.

'I want to go *home*,' she said, hanging back from the school door.

Mum looked as if she might relent. 'I don't see you two learning much in this sort of environment,' she whispered. 'Your dad's going to kill me when he finds out.'

'Let's just leg it back across the playground,' I said.

We looked at Mum pleadingly. She bit her lip, swaying from one Scholl sandal to the other, plucking helplessly at the roses on her hips. 'I don't know what to do for the best,' she said.

Then a man with black hair and a little beard

came up to us. He was wearing a denim jacket and black jeans, and he had a diamond earring in one lobe. We looked at him uncertainly. He seemed very young but the beard surely meant he couldn't be one of the pupils.

'Can I help?' he said.

'My girls are starting at the school. Well, I *think* they are,' said Mum.

He smiled at Grace and me. I usually couldn't stick men with beards but his was small and trimmed and looked cool, especially with the earring.

'I hope you'll be very happy here. Don't look so worried. It's always a bit weird starting at a new school.'

'They've not been to any school, not for years and years,' said Mum, starting to launch into a long and unnecessary resumé of our lives.

He listened politely while Grace and I rolled our eyes at each other, agonized.

'Well, I'm sure everything will be fine,' he interrupted eventually. He nodded at Grace and me. 'I'll maybe see you in the art room sometime. I'm Mr Raxberry. I'm one of the art teachers here.'

'I'm rubbish at art but Prue is brilliant,' said Grace.

'I'm not,' I said, blushing.

'Yes, you are,' said Grace.

I had to shut up or we would have got stuck in a ludicrous pantomime routine.

Mr Raxberry glanced at me. He had a very

intent way of looking, as if he was actually drawing me, noting everything about me. I wished I didn't look such a total idiot in my tablecloth dress. His dark eyes seemed very warm and sympathetic, as if he understood exactly what I was thinking.

He showed us to the office and introduced us to one of the school secretaries. 'Gina will look after you. Good luck! I hope you enjoy your first day,' he said, and then went hurrying off down the corridor.

Gina stared after him wistfully. She would obviously have preferred to look after *him*. She gave us forms to fill in and then told us to wait on chairs outside the headteacher's study.

We crouched there, all three of us, totally unnerved, while great gangs of students careered up and down the corridors, laughing, calling, shouting.

'Why don't the teachers tell them off?' Mum whispered. 'Still, the teachers seem a pretty rum lot. Imagine, that Mr Raxberry had an *earring*. You wouldn't think they'd allow it.'

'He teaches *art*, Mum,' I said.

'I don't know what your dad would say.'

There was a little pause. We were all horribly aware that Dad couldn't manage to say two words together at the moment.

I hunched up on my hard chair, guilt stabbing me in the stomach. Grace reached out sympathetically, and smudged the ink where she'd written her name on her form.

'Oh rats,' she said, sighing.

'Grace! Don't make it all messy,' said Mum. 'Do your name again, and try to keep your writing neat. Look, it's all over the place. Make it smaller, to fit on the line.'

'It won't *go* smaller,' said Grace, gripping her pen so tightly her knuckles went white. She stuck her tongue out as she wrote, concentrating fiercely. Then she peered at my form. 'Oh no! I've done my address wrong. I've mixed up the postcode letters,' she wailed. 'Shall I copy it out?'

'No, it'll look even more of a mess. Just leave it. As if it matters!' I said, though I'd written mine in my neatest printing, using my fine-line black drawing pen.

A smart blonde woman in a black trouser suit and high-heeled boots walked past us into the headteacher's office without even knocking.

'What a nerve! We were here first,' said Mum. 'Do you think she's his secretary?'

She wasn't the secretary. She put her head back round the door in two minutes and beckoned us in. She was the headteacher, Miss Wilmott.

'We didn't think you'd be a woman,' Mum said stupidly.

'Well, I promise you I'm not a man in drag, Mrs King,' she said.

Mum looked dreadfully embarrassed. Grace and I sniggered uncomfortably.

'Welcome to Wentworth,' said Miss Wilmott. 'We're all new girls together. I've only been here since the beginning of term.'

She indicated three chairs in front of her desk. She sat behind it, resting on her elbows, her hands crossed in front of her. They were very pretty hands with beautifully shaped nails, pink with bright white tips, as perfect as a porcelain doll.

Mum hid her own bunch-of-bananas hands in her floral lap. Grace sat on her own bitten fingernails. I made myself sit with my hands by my sides, pretending to be relaxed. I looked past Miss Wilmott at the paintings on her wall. They were mostly creation myths, but I recognized one Nativity scene, with a host of angels flying round above the stable, playing a heavenly version of 'Ring-a-ring-a-roses'. The painting had been in the same room as Tobias and his angel.

Miss Wilmott saw me staring. 'Do you like my painting? It's Italian, by Bellini.'

'No, it isn't!' I said, astonished. 'It's a Botticelli. He paints very differently, in a very poetic and ethereal way. I just adore his work.'

'I'm so pleased,' said Miss Wilmott, though she didn't sound pleased at all.

'She's very into art, our Prudence,' said Mum. 'My husband takes both girls to all the galleries, fills them in on all the details. He's taken such pains with them.'

'Excellent,' said Miss Wilmott briskly. 'Well, I'm determined there's going to be a big emphasis on the arts in Wentworth. I'm sure your daughters will appreciate their art lessons.'

'Oh, not me!' said Grace. 'I don't want to do art, thanks, because I'm useless at it. I'll just do English and history and geography and some nature stuff, but not anything hard.'

'You'll be given a timetable, Grace,' said Miss Wilmott. 'You'll find you'll be doing all sorts of subjects. But first of all, I'd like both of you to do a little test for me so we can sort out which year group to put you in.'

'I can't do tests,' said Grace anxiously, seemingly determined to convince Miss Wilmott she was totally bonkers.

'She panics,' Mum said. 'She's not really that clever – she takes after me, poor girl.' She laughed a false little ha-ha-ha. 'Prudence is the bright one,' Mum continued. 'She'll be top of her class, no problem.'

Miss Wilmott's smile was getting strained. 'We'll have the girls do their assessment tests and then we'll see,' she said. 'Meanwhile, Mrs King, I'd like to remind you that we do have a very strict uniform policy. Can you make sure the girls are kitted out in the regulation green uniform, please?'

'Oh yes, I've got that all in hand. They're going to buy their uniform at the special shop,' Mum said.

'I see,' said Miss Wilmott. She paused delicately. 'Are you on benefits, Mrs King? We do have an excellent free school lunch if that's the case.'

'Oh no, they'll take a packed lunch,' said Mum.

'We're not on any benefits at all, thank you.' Her cheeks were burning.

Miss Wilmott had no idea how she'd insulted her. She'd never heard one of Dad's rants about the Great Unwashed living off the State. Maybe Miss Wilmott thought *we* were the Great Unwashed, and possibly barking mad to boot. Her perfectly manicured nails were starting to fidget impatiently.

'Right then. We'll get Prudence and Grace settled in. School finishes at three thirty.' She gave Mum one more tight smile of dismissal.

Mum sat still, smiling back, not understanding. Grace sat gawping too.

'I won't have to do running or jumping or any games, will I?' Grace said.

'You'll have a games lesson twice a week. I think you'll find it fun,' said Miss Wilmott, getting up.

'But I can't, I've got a bad heart,' said Grace, putting her hand on her chest in a theatrical gesture.

I stared at her. She didn't have anything wrong with her heart. She could obviously lie as fluently as me when she was desperate enough.

Mum blinked at Grace, wondering what she was on about. Miss Wilmott didn't look convinced.

'If you want exemption from games you'll have to bring a letter from your doctor,' she said. 'But I'm sure a little gentle exercise won't do you any harm at all. Now, I really have to go to assembly. I'll settle you down with your tests, girls. Goodbye, Mrs King.'

Even Mum couldn't fail to get the message that it was time to go. She heaved herself upwards and gazed at Grace and me. Her eyes brimmed with tears but she did her best to smile. 'Have a nice day then, girls,' she said. 'I'll be waiting for you in the playground after school.'

'*No*, Mum, we'll walk home ourselves,' I said.

'Well, take great care, dear. Make sure you mind the roads and don't talk to strangers.'

She was treating us as if we were six. It was a relief when she waddled off down the corridor. She turned to wave at us again and again, as if she thought this was the last time she'd see us.

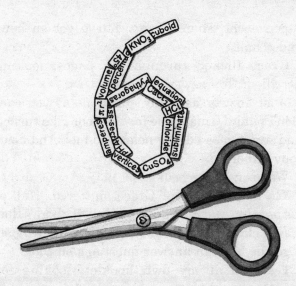

Grace and I sat at adjacent desks in a small room in a special unit called the Success Maker. Another girl sat at the back with some sort of helper. She was stumbling through an early reader book, spelling out the simplest words, often getting them wrong. Two foreign boys were with another teacher. He was making slow, deliberate conversation with them. 'Hello. My name is Mr Evans. I am thirty years old,' he said, expecting them to reciprocate. The boys mumbled and fidgeted, looking round the room, baffled.

I squeezed Grace's hand reassuringly under cover of the desks. She could speak English, she could read fluently. She didn't need to look so worried.

Gina gave us both booklets of questions and

a pen each. 'There we go. You've got an hour and a half.'

Grace flicked through the pages, looking horrified. 'To answer all *this*?'

'Just answer as many questions as you can. Don't panic.' Gina made for the door. She turned and saw Grace edging nearer to me. 'And don't copy either!'

We opened our booklets.

'Oh help help help!' Grace muttered. 'Half of it's *puzzles*. And mixed-up words. Oh, there's that spring cleaning bit from *The Wind in the Willows* – goodie, we can answer questions on *that*.'

I stared at my own booklet, looking for acrostics and anagrams and Moley in his burrow. I couldn't find them. My booklet was full of meaningless mathematical diagrams and sinister scientific formulae. My heart started thumping.

We had different booklets. Grace had one for eleven-year-olds just entering the school. Mine was for fourteen-year-olds starting Year Ten. I didn't know any of the answers. I was as hesitant as the girl reader, as baffled as the two boys. I stared at the paper long after Grace started scribbling away, her exuberant handwriting sloping wildly up and down the page.

I was so unnerved by the maths and the science that I was unsettled by the general intelligence questions too. I could see most of the missing sequences, fill in all the bracketed words, work out every code – but perhaps they were all trick questions? I dithered and crossed out and agonized, then decided to leave them and go back to them afterwards.

There was a passage of Shakespeare, unacknowledged, but it was the balcony scene from *Romeo and Juliet* so it was pretty obvious. I couldn't believe the question. *Do you think this scene was written recently? Give reasons for your answer.* Maybe this was a trick too? I decided to write a proper essay for Miss Wilmott to show her I wasn't a total moron.

I wrote three pages about Shakespeare and his times and the feud between the Montagues and the Capulets. I commented on the difference between courtship in Elizabethan times and nowadays, though I knew little about girl/boy relationships in my own time. It had been love at first sight for Romeo and Juliet. She was only fourteen, my age. I tried to imagine falling so headily, instantly in love that I would risk everything and kill myself if I couldn't be with my beloved.

I conjured up Tobias and wondered what it would be like if he stayed with me until sunrise. I wondered what he'd say, what he'd do . . .

I started violently when a very loud alarm bell rang and rang. I jumped up and grabbed Grace, looking round wildly for flames and smoke. But it wasn't a fire alarm, it was simply the school bell.

'It's break time now,' said Gina, bustling back. 'Time's up, girls. Pass your booklets to me.'

'But I haven't finished! I haven't done any of the stuff on the last two pages,' Grace wailed.

'Never mind. It's not like a real exam. It's just so we can assess you properly,' said Gina, snatching the booklet away from Grace.

I hugged mine tightly to my chest, feeling sick. I'd done far worse than Grace. I'd answered only a quarter of the questions. I just had to hope my essay would be taken into account.

I felt I'd let Dad down. I saw his face screw up with rage and frustration as he tried to berate me.

'There's no need to look so tragic,' Gina said to me. 'I'm sure you've done very well, dear. You've written heaps.'

I'd written heaps of rubbish. I was put in a remedial class.

They didn't *call* it that. It was simply Form 10 EL. I pondered the significance of EL. Extreme Losers? Educationally Lacking? Evidently Loopy? I discovered they were merely the initials of our form teacher, Eve Lambert. But it was obvious that we were the sad guys in the school, the hopeless cases. Some could barely speak English and were traumatized, looking round fearfully as if they expected a bomb to go off any minute. Others were loud and disruptive, standing up and swearing. One boy couldn't sit still at all and fidgeted constantly, biting his fingernails and flipping his ruler and folding the pages in his notebook. He hummed all the time like a demonic bee. Most of my fellow pupils seemed scarily surly. The only girl who gave me a big smile had obvious learning difficulties.

I was the girl supposedly intellectually gifted. This was the class considered appropriate for my abilities. It was totally humiliating to find I could barely keep up. It was like being back with Miss Roberts, only worse. I still couldn't get to grips with maths, though the teacher spoke very s-l-o-w-l-y and CLEARLY, as if superior enunciation would enlighten everybody.

Science was only a fraction easier. I thought I would do well in history and geography but I was used to reading a book and then imagining what an era or a country would be like. I hated this school approach where everything was divided up into topics and you needed to memorize little gobbets of information.

I found French hard too, though I knew enough of it to guess my way through simple books. I discovered I mispronounced all the words. When I was asked to recite the numbers between one and twenty the class started sniggering as I said each number. By the time I said *dix-huit* as 'dicks-hewitt' they were in tears of laughter.

I hoped English would be my saving grace, but I didn't like the teacher, Mrs Godfrey, at all. She looked stylish, tall and thin, almost like a fashion model, and she wore black, with big black glasses framing her dark eyes. She was alarmingly strict, making sarcastic comments about all of us, even the clearly unfortunate.

She told us to write about a poem, 'Adlestrop'. I knew it by heart already so I cheered up. I knew I could write *pages*. I didn't have anything to write *in*, so I went up to Mrs Godfrey's desk at the front of the classroom.

'Feel free to wander at will around my classroom,' she said.

I gathered I *shouldn't* feel free. I didn't know what to do. She didn't look up from her marking. I shifted from one foot to another, not sure how to address her. She made dismissive waving gestures at me while I was making up my mind.

'I haven't got an English exercise book,' I blurted out.

She sighed. 'I haven't got an English exercise book, *Mrs Godfrey*,' she repeated. 'So what have you done with your English exercise book? Have you torn it into strips and scattered it down the lavatory? Have you hurled it frisbee-fashion over the nearest hedge? Have you fed it to a goat for breakfast?'

The class were sniggering again. I waited, crimson-cheeked, for her to complete her comedy routine. She looked up at last.

'What is your name?'

'Prudence King.'

'Prudence King, *Mrs Godfrey*!'

I repeated the ridiculous phrase.

'And you've mislaid your English exercise book?'

'I've never *owned* an English exercise book,' I said. '*Mrs Godfrey*,' I added, emphasizing her name.

This didn't please her. Her eyes glittered behind her glasses. 'Are you being intentionally insolent?' she asked.

I wasn't, but *she* certainly was. I wanted to slap her. She gave me a wretched exercise book and dismissed me back to my desk with another imperious wave of her long white fingers.

I couldn't understand why she was being so deliberately unkind. I decided I'd show *her*. I started writing reams on 'Adlestrop' – and lots of other Edward Thomas poems, bringing in some of the First World War poets too, and mentioning Helen Thomas's lovely book *As It Was*, which I'd found in a dusty corner of the biography section in the shop this summer. I'd read the bit where Helen and Edward go to bed in a lavender-smelling four-poster in a country inn again and again. I had just enough sense to leave this bit out of my essay, but I put everything else in, my hand hurtling down the page.

I thought we'd have to hand our books in to be marked but after twenty minutes or so Mrs Godfrey clapped her hands and went to sit on top of her desk, her long legs dangling, her feet elegant in black high heels.

'Right, class, who shall beguile us first?' she said. 'Daisy, perhaps you'd like to read out your essay?'

Daisy was a very large girl with wild tufty hair. 'Ooh not me, miss, I can't, miss, don't want to,' she said, giggling bashfully.

I could understand why she didn't want to when she read her piece out loud.

'"This is a poem about this place called Adlestrop. It sounds like a nice place. It's a short poem. It's got some funny words like unwontedly."'

That was *it*. I expected Mrs Godfrey to stamp all over her with her high heels, but she was relatively kind.

'Short, but sweet, Daisy,' she said. 'There's no harm in being concise.' She peered over at my scribbled pages and raised her eyebrows. 'All right, Prudence King, perhaps you'd like to share your words of wisdom with us?'

My hands were shaking but I read in a loud clear voice to show her she didn't really scare me. The class started sniggering again. I didn't understand why. This wasn't French. I knew how to pronounce all the words. I only realized why after I'd heard the others mumble through their pieces. It clearly wasn't the done thing to project your voice and read with expression. It was as embarrassing as my tablecloth frock. Even Mrs Godfrey had a smirk on her face.

'That's enough,' she said, long before I'd reached my conclusion. 'It's very kind of you to share your erudition with us lowly mortals, Prudence King, but I think we've had a tad more information than we can absorb.'

So that was it. I couldn't win. I was humiliated in maths and science by my ignorance, ridiculed in French for my mispronunciation, and mocked in English for my enthusiasm.

All right then, I thought. I wouldn't say a word more. I sat silently throughout the rest of the English lesson, refusing to join in a general discussion of 'Adlestrop'. I tried to hold my head high to show I couldn't care less, but it made my neck ache. I was so miserable I was on the verge of tears.

The last two lessons were devoted to PE. I relaxed a little. I was small and strong and whippy. I could run like the wind and catch any ball. I didn't know how to play any sporty games like netball and hockey but I was sure I could learn soon enough.

I followed the others to the gym and found the girls' changing room. Then the obvious dawned on me. I didn't have any PE kit.

The PE teacher, Miss Peters, came bounding up in her pale grey tracksuit, her whistle bouncing on her chest. I steeled myself for another sarcastic charade, but Miss Peters smiled at me with genuine warmth.

'Hello! What's your name then? Prudence? Ah, I love those old-fashioned names. I'm Miss Peters. Is this your first day at Wentworth? Bit of a culture shock, I expect. Right, Prudence, get yourself changed, lickety spit, there's a good girl.'

'I can't,' I said. 'I haven't got anything to change into.'

'You haven't got any old shorts and a T-shirt?' said Miss Peters. 'Oh well, never mind, I've got heaps of spares in my lost property basket, so nil desperandum. There, you learn Latin as a bonus in my PE lessons.'

She handed me someone else's off-white shirt and crumpled green shorts. I clutched them unwillingly, looking round the benches and pegs in the changing room. I couldn't see any cubicles.

'Where do you get changed, please?' I asked.

'Here!' said Miss Peters, waving her arm to indicate the room.

Sure enough the girls were starting to take off their school blouses and skirts as casually as if they were in their own private bedroom. I stared at them, astonished. I didn't even undress like that in front of Grace.

I started undoing my tablecloth frock down the front. It had a zip at the side so it clung too tightly to wriggle out of decorously. I always had to pull it up and over my head. My heart started thudding underneath the red and white checks.

I looked round wildly and saw a toilet sign. I grabbed my things and started shuffling towards it.

'Where are you off to, Prudence?' Miss Peters asked.

'The loo,' I said.

She was way ahead of me. 'Sorry, Prudence, we let Shanaz and Gurpreet change in the toilets, but I'm afraid the rest of you aren't allowed to be modest. Don't worry, we're all girls together – and nobody's looking at you anyway.'

Correction! They were *all* looking at me. I didn't know what to do. I just stood there foolishly, very very slowly unbuttoning and unzipping.

'Prudence, do get a move on,' Miss Peters called. She paused, arms akimbo, waiting.

I couldn't delay any more. She might come and rip my frock off herself if I didn't watch out.

I picked up my hem and tugged. I tried to whip my dress off immediately but my long hair got tangled in the zip. I was stuck with my head swathed in red-checked cotton, my underwear on display to everyone.

'My God, look what the new girl's wearing!'

'It's a *thong!*'

'She's wearing slag's knickers to school!'

'Bright pink lace – oh my God!'

I pulled my hair hard and tore my dress off.

'She's got the bra to match though she's hardly got any boobs to fit into it!'

'Where did you buy your underwear, Prudence? Ann Summers?'

'Who'd have thought it! She looks such a nerdy snob in that mad dress too. Wait till we tell the boys!'

I pulled on my borrowed top and shorts in a panic. Miss Peters shook her head at me as I sidled past her.

'You're at *school*, Prudence. It's plain bra and big knickers in future, OK?'

My face was as pink as my lace pants. I felt they were glowing luridly through my shorts

77

and shirt. Everyone was looking at me, whispering and giggling.

I felt so bewildered. I thought this was the sort of underwear all these streetwise scary girls had been wearing since they were ten years old.

I was so flustered I couldn't concentrate when Miss Peters told me the basic rules of netball. I caught the ball, no bother, but kept running with it. I couldn't understand why people shouted at me when I rushed up to the net and scored a goal. Apparently it didn't count because I wasn't a shooter.

I didn't try after that. I shuffled aimlessly after all the others, not knowing what I was doing, not caring. I tried to imagine Jane running along beside me, but she backed away in horror and went to read her book in the corner. Tobias looked embarrassed for me in my hideous shorts and ambled off on his own. I was left lurching my way through the lesson, friendless.

It was torture getting changed back into my dress when the bell went. Everyone was all set to have another laugh at my underwear. I waited until I was the last girl in the changing room and then whipped my dress on quick.

I was worried about Grace. She'd be waiting for me at the school gate, wondering where I'd got to. I was supposed to go back to the classroom to collect my new books from my desk. I'd been set several pieces of homework. I wasn't sure how to find my way back down all the corridors. I decided I couldn't be bothered. I was determined never to come back to this terrible school so there was no point attempting any of the homework.

I rushed out of the door and peered across the playground. I saw a patch of pink way over at the school gate, but it was sandwiched between two regulation green blobs. I hurried towards them, wondering if Grace was being picked on. She saw me coming and waved – an idiotic exaggerated gesture, waggling both hands. The girl either side of her waved double-handed too. I approached them warily. They grinned at me like three monkeys.

'Hi, Prue! These are my friends, Iggy and Figgy,' Grace gabbled.

'I'm Jean Igloo,' said Iggy, baring her braces. She gave a mock shiver and mimed a dome in case I hadn't quite caught on.

'I'm Fiona Harrison,' said Figgy, flicking her long limp hair away from her long limp face. 'I've been Figgy ever since I made friends with Iggy. Plus I love figgy pudding, yum.'

'I'm Piggy,' Grace announced proudly.

She didn't need to explain. She did anyway, puffing out her cheeks and patting her fat stomach. I wanted to die for her but she seemed thrilled to bits with her new name.

I wondered if Iggy and Figgy had simply made up this nickname rubbish on the spot and were all set to make a terrible fool of Grace, but they seemed such sad loser girls themselves it didn't seem likely. But then maybe I was an even sadder totally lost girl myself. I hadn't made any friends, not even two such pathetic girls as these.

They seemed genuinely fond of Grace, telling her she mustn't panic if she couldn't do her homework, because she could always copy off them. They both gave her their mobile phone numbers, and Grace gave them our home land phone number.

'Grace!' I said. 'What about Dad?' He would go demented if an Iggy or Figgy rang asking to speak to her. Then I remembered Dad was stuck in the stroke unit and currently unable to speak to anyone.

Grace looked at me and tapped her forehead, indicating I was mad. 'Dad isn't there,' she said.

'Yes, but we'll be out visiting him this evening.'

'Yeah, but, like, that's not going to take, like, all night,' said Grace, grinning at Iggy and Figgy.

She was talking like them already, raising her eyebrows and sighing as if *I* was the sad sister.

'Come on,' I said fiercely, grabbing hold of her by the wrist.

She wriggled away and did the maddening wave again. Iggy and Figgy did it too.

'What's with all this waving? You look a total idiot,' I hissed at her.

'It's our secret club wave,' Grace said.

'Oh yes, very secret, you're all so subtle when practising it,' I said. 'Correction. You look like *prats*.'

'Why are you being so horrible?' said Grace. 'I'm just trying to fit in and make friends. Isn't that what you're supposed to do when you go to school?'

'You could be a bit *selective* about your friends,' I said, miming the handwave, while bucking my teeth and flipping my hair.

'Don't,' said Grace, going red. 'I *like* Iggy and Figgy.'

'Yes, well, they obviously *don't* like you, calling you Piggy. That's a hateful nickname.'

'It was my idea, not theirs. It's not hateful, it's funny. I think you're just jealous because I've made two friends and you haven't,' said Grace.

She saw me wince. 'Yeah, it looks like you've been *too* selective,' she said.

'I wouldn't want to be friends with anyone at this stupid school. I hate everyone in it. I don't intend to come back here ever,' I said.

I started running. I dashed into the road, not thinking where I was going, acting like a crazy person. There was a squeal of brakes and a loud honking of a car horn. I stopped still, disorientated, feeling a total fool. Grace was screaming in shock behind me and some guy was winding down his car window, ready to shout at me.

He didn't shout. He shook his head at me and said softly, 'You must be in a hurry to get home.'

It was Mr Raxberry, the art teacher.

'I'm sorry, I just wasn't looking,' I stammered.

I turned round to Grace. 'Stop that screaming!'

'I though you were going to be killed!' Grace whimpered.

'I did too!' said Mr Raxberry. 'But I try not to make a habit of exterminating my pupils, especially on their first day at Wentworth. Get back on the pavement before another car comes along and really knocks you flying.'

I shuffled back to the kerb, still feeling incredibly stupid, but pleased he was being so sweet about it. I thought he'd drive off but he parked the car beside us.

I squeezed Grace's hand to calm her down, and show her I was really sorry for being so mean. She squeezed back and stayed clinging to me.

Mr Raxberry smiled at us both. 'How did it go then, girls?' he asked.

'It was OK!' said Grace. 'I've got these two friends, Iggy and Figgy and—'

'Grace,' I interrupted, scared she was going to go through the whole Iggy-Figgy-Piggy saga all over again.

'We're friends,' Grace persisted. 'They're going to help me because I don't know heaps of stuff. Still, the teachers say I'll soon catch up as I'm still just in the first term.'

'That's great,' said Mr Raxberry. Then he looked at me. 'What about you, Prue?'

He remembered my name!

I didn't know what to say, so I simply shrugged.

'Oh dear,' he said. 'Yep. That was *my* reaction

my first day here. In fact I often feel that way now. But it'll get easier, you'll see. And I think your class is due an art lesson tomorrow. We can check each other out then. Bye now.'

He drove off, waving. I stared after him until his car had gone right down the road and round the corner.

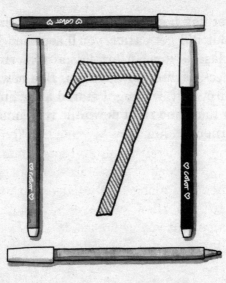

Mum was waiting for us at the bookshop door, rushing out to hug us extravagantly as if we'd just escaped from a bear pit. It *felt* as if I had been bitten by sharp ursine teeth and clawed by big paws. Still, it was so comforting to know that Mr Raxberry understood. Did he really get anxious too? He looked so cool and laid-back with his casual jeans and his earring. It seemed almost impossible. And he was a *teacher*, for goodness' sake. No one could pick on him, tell him off or tease him. Mum wanted to hear all about our day, minute by minute. I couldn't face telling her any of it so I pretended I had to go and get on with homework straight away. I left Grace Iggying and Figgying, munching strawberry jam sponge cake, her mouth red and glistening as if she was wearing lipstick.

I sat cross-legged on my bed, my sketchpad on my lap. I *did* have heaps of homework but as I'd left it all at school I decided to forget about it. I started drawing instead, scribbling any old thing with my felt tips, just seeing what I could jot down. I drew me wearing a real square tablecloth, running like crazy, my hair flying out behind me, my mouth wide and screaming. I was pursued by a pack of bottle-green bears. I drew a car creeping along at the edge of the page, ready to run them all over. I shaded the windscreen, but you could see dark hair, a little beard and the tiny glint of an earring.

I was left in peace until half past five, when Mum closed the shop. She hadn't had a single customer all afternoon, but she still waited until it was five thirty on the dot, carefully consulting her watch.

'Come on then, girls, off to see your father,' she said.

We stared at her pleadingly.

'Mum, do we have to go every day?' I said.

'Of course we do!' Mum said. 'Think of your poor father lying there, waiting and waiting for us. How on earth would he feel if we couldn't be bothered to come? Besides, I've got his clean pyjamas, and a big slice of sponge cake to perk him up.'

'But Mum, Iggy and Figgy are going to be phoning me to see how I'm getting on with my homework – which I'm *not*; it's, like, *way* too difficult,' said Grace, raising her eyebrows and trying out a weird shrugging gesture.

'Stop twitching like that, Grace. And talk *properly*. Don't start talking like that in front of your father, you know it will infuriate him.'

'Everything I do infuriates him,' said Grace. 'It will probably make him worse seeing me. He won't mind a bit if you and Prue go and I stay at home. He'd definitely *prefer* it.'

I glared at her. I didn't want to get lumbered going with Mum while Grace escaped. 'I annoy him too. It was me that made him have the stroke in the first place,' I said.

'Don't, Prue,' said Mum. 'That's nonsense, I'm sure you had nothing to do with it. Come on, get ready, both of you. And don't breathe a word to your dad about going to school – that really will set him off.'

So we walked into town and caught the bus to the hospital. When we got there Dad was fast asleep, snoring, his mouth open, his false teeth slipping sideways over his lip so he looked like Dracula. We drew up chairs beside him and waited for him to wake up.

'Shall I give him a shake?' I said.

'Well, it seems a shame when he's so peaceful,' said Mum. She seemed content to watch him, as if he was a television. Grace and I wriggled on our orange plastic chairs. Dad didn't seem at all peaceful to me. He mumbled and groaned in his sleep, his good left arm and leg twitching. I wondered if he was walking and talking in his dream, unaffected by the stroke.

It must be so awful for him to wake up imprisoned in his half-dead body, unable to say the simplest thing. I felt so sorry for him that I leaned forward and took hold of his bad hand. I touched the limp fingers, as if I could somehow squeeze the life back into them.

Dad's eyes shot open. I dropped his hand quickly. I tried desperately to think of something to say to him.

'Hello. It's me, Dad. Prue. Well, obviously. How are you? Sorry, that's a stupid thing to say.' I was speaking as if I was the one with speech difficulties.

Dad tried to reply, his face screwed up with the effort, a vein standing out on his forehead like a big blue worm crawling under his skin. 'I want . . .' he said, in a new strange thick voice. 'I want . . .'

He couldn't manage to say what he wanted. Mum kept trying to interpret.

'Yes, Bernard? What do you want? A drink of water? A cup of tea? Do you need the toilet, dear?'

Dad groaned and thumped his good left hand on the mattress in frustration. One of the very few words he had left was a very rude term of abuse. He repeated it explosively, saliva glistening on his lips, as if he was spewing bile with his awful insult.

'Ooh, you naughty boy, Mr King,' Nurse Ray said, flitting past.

Dad said it louder, while Mum flushed, blood flooding right down her neck and across her chest.

'He doesn't know what he's saying, poor lamb,' she said quickly.

Dad obviously knew exactly what he was saying. He said it louder still.

It was so sad we wanted to cry, but it was embarrassingly funny too. Grace and I suddenly started spluttering with laughter. We put our hands over our mouths and bit our cheeks, but couldn't control it. Mum was furious with us.

'How dare you mock your father when he's so poorly!' she hissed.

We apologized meekly, but we couldn't catch each other's eye without collapsing. Mum glared at us and produced the slice of sponge cake, making 'yum-yum' noises and licking gestures. She tucked it into Dad's left hand but he tossed it indifferently onto the bedcovers.

'Can't you eat it, dear? Shall I break it up into mouthfuls, would that be easier? Come on, Bernard, you like my special sponge cake.'

'Can I have some, Mum?' Grace asked.

'Of course not! It's for your dad,' said Mum.

'But he's not hungry,' said Grace. She nodded across at his supper tray, still barely touched, though the sandwiches were starting to curl and the sliced banana on his bowl of yoghurt was going brown. 'Can I finish his sandwiches then?'

'No! It's a disgrace – that nurse should have seen to him. He obviously can't manage by himself.'

Mum complained bitterly behind the nurses' backs, but couldn't steel herself to say anything at all to their faces. When Nurse Ray popped her head round the door I dared mumble that perhaps my dad needed to be fed at meal times.

She roared with laughter. 'We've tried that lark, dearie. He spat gravy and mash all over my apron front. He'll eat if he wants to. His left hand's fine, and if he'd only co-operate with our physiotherapist his right hand could get back into some sort of working order.'

Dad said his rude word again when she said the word physiotherapist. Nurse Ray laughed, shaking her head at him.

'Yes, you've fallen out with her, haven't you, Mr King!' She turned to us. 'He won't let us dress him in his shorts, and yet the physio needs to see his legs properly to check the right muscles are working.'

'My husband's never been keen on shorts,' Mum apologized.

'Maybe you'd like to try to get him to practise his exercises? Little and often! These first three months are vital. He needs pretty intensive speech therapy too. His vocabulary is pretty limited at the moment.'

Dad said his swearword again.

'Mr King! Don't say that naughty word in front of your wife and daughters!' Nurse Ray said, pretending to be shocked.

'You could help your dad, Prue,' said Mum. 'You could teach him to say new words.'

'*Respectable* words!' said Nurse Ray, giggling.

'I – I don't know how to,' I said lamely.

'Just chatter to him same as always, darling, and then try to get him to say stuff back,' she said.

I'd never chattered to Dad in my life. He'd always interrupted us. 'Is there any *point* to this story?' he'd say. 'Or are you just in love with the sound of your own voice?'

Dad was the one who always commandeered the conversation. My mouth dried as I tried to think of something to say.

'I've got two new friends, Dad,' Grace said unexpectedly. 'Iggy and Figgy.'

'Shut *up*, Grace!' Mum said sharply.

'It's OK, I'm not going to mention you-know-what. I'm just going to tell him about my friends. Can you say Iggy, Dad? Can you say Figgy? They're easy words.'

Dad didn't try.

'Maybe you'd like to try ultra difficult words,' I said suddenly. 'Like . . . antidisestablishment-arianism?'

Dad had told us that this was the longest word in the English language. He stared at me. His face wobbled and a weird howling sound came out of his sideways mouth. He was laughing!

'An-ti,' he said. 'An-ti.'

'Yeah, ant et cetera, et cetera, et cetera,' I said. 'Or maybe you'd like foreign words? I know. Tell me the name of an Italian Renaissance painter.'

Dad struggled. 'Bot,' he said. 'Bot – bot-bot.'

'Botticelli,' I said. 'Yay! You're not only talk-ing, Dad, you're talking Italian.' Dad thought hard, his brow wrinkled. 'Spag,' he said.

'Spaghetti!' I said.

Dad nodded, but he wasn't finished. Saliva dribbled down his chin. 'Spag *bol*,' he said.

'Spaghetti bolognese, what else?' I said. 'I bet you'd nosh on a plateful of spag bol if they'd serve it up to you!'

Dad frowned. 'No – *nosh*,' he said, prodding at me with his good hand.

He'd always hated any slang. For once I didn't mind him nagging about it. It was such a relief to know that Dad was exactly the same inside – even though I'd longed all my life for him to change.

I gave him a kiss on the cheek when we said goodbye. He batted me away furiously, but he didn't call me the bad word.

'You've always been able to handle your dad,' Mum sighed, as we trailed home from the bus stop.

She was wearing her comfiest shoes, awful boy's lace-ups she found at a jumble sale, but she still lagged behind Grace and me. She was breathing heavily, shuffling Dad's dirty laundry bag from hand to hand.

'Here, Mum, let me carry it,' I said, ashamed.

'That's nice of you, dear,' Mum panted. 'Let me take your arm. You come the other side, Grace. There, isn't that cosy?'

It was anything but. I hated lumbering down the street linked to my mum and sister. I felt a total fool.

'I'll run on home and get the kettle on for a cup of tea for you, Mum,' I said, breaking free.

The telephone was ringing as I got the door open. It always unnerved me. It hardly ever rang. Had Dad had a sudden relapse?

I snatched up the phone and said hello anxiously.

'Hi, Piggy!' two voices squealed in unison.

'Oh for heaven's *sake*. OK, hang on a minute, she's coming down the road,' I said.

I hollered out the door to Grace. She came thudding down the street, cheeks bright pink, her pale eyelashes fluttering, looking alarmingly aptly nicknamed.

She was still on the phone long after Mum had had two cups of tea.

'Do say goodbye now, dear, it'll be costing Iggy's or Figgy's folk a fortune,' she said. She looked pleased, even so. 'Isn't it lovely Grace has made two friends already?' she said.

I barely responded.

'You'll make friends soon too, Prudence, just you wait and see,' said Mum.

'I don't *want* to make friends,' I said.

I knew I sounded pathetic. I stole up to my bedroom, stared at my bear pit drawing and suddenly crumpled it up because it looked so weird and stupid.

I lay on the bed, my face buried in my pillow. Jane came and lay beside me, nestling up close. She understood without my having to say a word. She'd attended Lowood School. She knew how awful it could be. But even Jane had found a friend, Helen Burns. I had no one.

Grace came bouncing up to bed, going on and on about Iggy and Figgy. I pulled the covers over my head.

'Prue?'

I wouldn't answer. I hoped she'd think I'd gone to sleep, even though I was still fully dressed in my terrible tablecloth frock.

'Oh Prue, you're not crying, are you?' said Grace, thumping down on the bed beside me. Her hand squirmed under the duvet. She patted me like a puppy. 'I know, it's so batty, me being the one to like school and make friends and stuff, but it's easier for me. I'm in Year Seven so we're *all* new. And I'm all silly and smiley so people can see I *want* to be friends.'

I couldn't bear Grace being so kind and understanding. Her sympathy somehow made things worse. I still wouldn't talk to her.

I lay awake for hours, hating myself for being such a mean sister. No wonder no one liked me.

'I like you,' Tobias whispered.

Jane had long since stolen away in her shabby button boots, but Tobias was there in the dark, holding my hand. He told me that he liked me precisely because I was strange and passionate and peculiar. He said all the girls in my form were banal and ordinary by comparison.

'I wish there was a boy in my form just like you, Tobias,' I whispered.

8

I felt sick when I woke up the next morning. I decided to stick to my original plan and not go back to school at all. What did I care about Mr Raxberry and his art lesson? He might be sweet to me but everyone else was so awful. Why should I put myself through such horrors?

I could walk to school with Grace and then keep on walking right into town. I didn't have any money to spend but I could window shop or go and browse in the library or walk in the park.

I packed my shoulder bag with sketchbook, crayons and my well-thumbed copy of *Jane Eyre* to keep me going all day long.

'Are you reading *Jane Eyre* in your class?' Grace asked. 'How lovely for you, as it's your favourite book! I bet you'll be top in English, and art, and everything else. I think I'm nearly at the bottom but at least Dad won't know and get mad at me. And Iggy and Figgy aren't, like, total brain boxes. Figgy kept getting the wrong answer in maths yesterday, but she didn't care a bit, she just got the giggles.' Grace giggled too just thinking about it.

I let her ramble on, deciding to keep quiet about my plans. I knew she'd worry and fuss. I didn't want her unwittingly giving me away to Mum.

But as we were walking down Wentworth Road there was a little toot of a car horn. I looked up and Mr Raxberry gave me a little wave.

'Is that the art teacher?' said Grace, as if she really wasn't sure.

'Yes!'

'He's quite nice,' said Grace vaguely. She was looking all around. Then she suddenly grinned maniacally, did her two-handed fool's wave, and scurried forwards on her fat little legs. There were Iggy and Figgy at the gate, grinning and waving back.

I told myself to walk on smartly past the school. Grace was so keen to see her silly new friends she'd barely notice. But somehow my feet in their old red strap shoes were marching me in through the gate.

I had to go. Mr Raxberry would be looking out for me. I didn't think he'd tell on me if I didn't turn up, but he'd maybe worry and wonder where I was. I didn't want to let him down when he'd been so kind to me. He was the

95

closest I'd got to a friend at Wentworth, even though he was one of the teachers.

I didn't know where to go meanwhile. I didn't want to hang around Grace on the periphery of the Iggy-Figgy-Piggy club. I wandered off across the playground, dazed by the shouting, the swearing, the pushing and shoving. I decided to find my way to my classroom and lose myself in *Jane Eyre* for ten minutes. I blundered up and down endless corridors, hopelessly lost. By the time I found it, the classroom was crowded, and there was no chance of slinking to my desk and burying myself in my book.

The girls all gathered round me. I couldn't get them sorted out as individuals, apart from big Daisy with the tufty hair, and smiley Sarah, the girl with learning difficulties. But they all knew who I was, of course.

'It's Posh Prue, in her red-checked tablecloth *again*!'

'Yuck!' said another, holding her nose. 'I couldn't *stick* wearing yesterday's dirty clothes.'

'She's too posh to wash,' someone giggled.

I hadn't realized that most people wore a clean outfit every day. Mum made Grace and me wear the same dress all week, unless we spilled something down it. Our ancient washing machine hadn't worked for months, so Mum had to lug great plastic bags down to the launderette or wash everything out by hand.

I decided to ignore their hostile remarks. I settled at my desk, got out my book and tried to read. The words wiggled up and down the page, refusing to convey any meaning. My eyes blurred. I prayed I wasn't going to burst into tears.

'Hey you, Posh Prue, we're talking to you!'

One girl jabbed at me with her long pointed nail. Another snatched at my skirt, trying to lift it.

'Stop it!' I said.

'Just wanted to see if you've got your slag's underwear on again, that's all.'

'Get off! Leave me alone!' I cried.

I hadn't thought to change my dress but I'd had the wit to leave my beautiful doomed lace underwear at home. However, I knew my substitute grey-white baggy knickers would be equally ridiculed. I was determined to keep them hidden, though four or five of the girls were now scrabbling at my hem, exposing my thighs.

'There are boys in the room, for God's sake!' I shrieked.

They all fell about laughing, making silly 'Ooooh!' cooing noises, like demented doves. One of the bigger boys was lounging on the teacher's desk, legs dangling. He looked over at us.

'Leave her alone, girlies,' he said.

They backed off immediately, giggling and grinning. I stared, surprised. He was the only boy in the class who was remotely good looking. He was tall and slim, with longish fair hair. He'd customized his school uniform, his shirt hanging loose, his sleeves rolled up, and he was wearing cool pointy boots instead of scuffed trainers like the other lads. It was obvious all the girls tormenting me fancied him like mad.

'So why have we got to back off?' said one of the girls. She was the fiercest, and probably the prettiest, with carefully curled dark hair and heavy black eye make-up like Cleopatra. She narrowed her outlined eyes at the boy. 'Are you waiting to have a shufty at the slag's underwear yourself, Toby?'

'Give it a rest, Rita,' he said, laughing at her.

He was called Toby! He did look just a little like my Tobias, though this was a real rough lad, not an ethereal boy with an angel for his best buddy.

I gave him a shy little nod. He winked at me and then carried on chatting to his mates. I knew he'd just taken pity on me. I was new and weird and hideous in my home clothes. He'd put me in the same category as smiley Sarah. He'd protected me automatically without even thinking about it.

It didn't look as if Rita saw it that way. She glared at me.

'Stupid little tart,' she hissed in my face. 'Don't you dare go making eyes at my Toby.'

'Don't worry about it,' I said, picking up *Jane Eyre* again.

My hands were shaking. I hoped they wouldn't notice. I dropped my book and hunted for my new timetable instead. I looked to see when I had an art lesson. It wasn't until the afternoon. It seemed as far away as Christmas. I had God knows how many terrible lessons to get through first, plus a session in the Success Maker.

It was the Portakabin we'd taken our tests in. It was clearly for pupils who were currently utterly *un*successful. Most of them were refugees, with an obvious excuse for their lack of ability in a completely foreign language. Even so, they mastered basic maths and science quicker than I did.

I was the worst student in the entire unit at IT. I couldn't even initially tell the difference between a television and a computer. Mr Widnes the tutor thought I was being deliberately insolent when I sat down in front of the unit television and struggled to switch it on.

'All right, Miss Clever Clogs, stop taking the mickey,' he said, sighing. Then he saw my expression. 'OK, you're obviously not into computers. But surely you've got a *television* at home.'

'We haven't, actually,' I said miserably.

It wasn't for want of trying. Grace and I had begged Dad year after year to let us have a set. Mum had stressed that it would be highly educational, and we'd just watch the arts and nature programmes.

'Educational, my bottom,' said Dad, though he'd put it more crudely. 'They'd just gawp at cartoons and sleazy rubbish – and you'd all get hooked on those wretched soaps.'

So we'd gone without, and consequently felt

more out of touch than ever with the modern world. Mr Widnes clearly thought I came from a bizarrely impoverished background and treated me very gently from then on. I was so stupid trying to do the most basic things and I couldn't even move the mouse around properly. His patience must have been severely tested.

It was a relief to escape the Success Maker at lunch time, but then I had to steel myself for English with Mrs Godfrey.

'Where's your English comprehension homework, Prudence King?'

'I haven't done it yet, Mrs Godfrey. I forgot to take my books home last night.'

I remembered to say her stupid name. I spoke politely. I still infuriated her.

'You don't "forget" to take your books home, Prudence King. Homework isn't a choice, it's compulsory at this school. You will do *two* comprehensions tonight, the one on page thirty-one *and* the one on page thirty-three, do you understand? Come and find me first thing tomorrow morning and hand in both completed exercises or you will find yourself in very serious trouble.'

I wondered what her very serious trouble could be. I thought of Jane Eyre, forced to stand on a table with a placard round her neck in front of all the other pupils at Lowood. I'd rather enjoy standing there like a martyr, gazing over their heads. I tried out an eyeballs-rolled martyr's gaze.

'Are you being deliberately insolent again, Prudence?' Mrs Godfrey said, flushing.

'No, Mrs Godfrey,' I said, lowering my eyes, though of course I *was*. She knew it, I knew it, the whole class knew it. Some of the tougher kids looked at me with a little more respect.

Mrs Godfrey noticed this, and went into serious rant mode. She asked me who on earth I thought I was, said she was sick of my attitude, stated that this was certainly not the way to start at a new school, etc. etc. It wasn't a full Dad-style rant, just an irritating bleat. I wondered why I annoyed her so much. I decided I was glad. How awful to be liked by someone so petty and arrogant and unfair.

I tried the trick I used whenever Dad flew into a terrible temper. I pretended I was in a suit of armour, with a helmet locked protectively over my face. I felt invincible inside my rigid silver suit. No one could get at me or hurt me or harm me.

I kept my armour on all through English and clanked along behind the other pupils when the bell went. It was time for the art lesson at last.

The art block was detached from the main building, in a special shack at the very end of the playing field. It took me a long while to get there. I trudged more and more slowly, as if I was truly clad in armour.

I looked longingly at the school gate. No one would notice if I slipped out now. It was so strange. The only reason I'd suffered this second

101

day of schooling was to attend Mr Raxberry's art class, and yet now I didn't want to go. I felt shy and stupid.

I didn't understand. I was *good* at art. Mr Raxberry wouldn't ridicule me like the repellent Mrs Godfrey. Mr Raxberry was kind. He was so different from all the other teachers. He didn't *act* like a teacher. He wasn't sarcastic or pompous or patronizing. He was gentle and funny and truthful and self-deprecating and sensitive. I could add any number of adjectives, even though I'd spoken to him so briefly. I could write an entire essay on him. I could write pages on a physical description of Mr Raxberry. I could paint his portrait, showing the way he tilted his head slightly, the wrinkles at the edge of his eyes, the softness of his white cheeks contrasted with the dark springiness of his small beard, the diamond earring in the centre of his neat earlobe . . .

I could conjure his exact image in front of my eyes, but I was scared of confronting the real Mr Raxberry. I ran my fingers through my long tangled hair, trying to comb it into submission. I plucked at my hideous dress. I put my hand against my cheeks and felt them burning. I hoped my nose wasn't shiny. I wished I could wear make-up like the other girls.

I wondered whether to trek back into school to find the girls' cloakrooms and check on myself in the mirror there. I was five minutes late for the lesson already.

I stood dithering, wondering why I was in such a ridiculous state. I took several deep breaths, trying to calm down. 'Go *on*!' I urged myself.

I imagined giant hands on my shoulders, pushing me forwards, frog-marching me to the art block. I stumbled along and got there at last, but I still couldn't force myself in the door.

I hung around outside, minute after minute ticking by. I could hear the sound of Mr Raxberry's voice, but not what he was saying. Every now and then the class murmured. Once they all burst out laughing. I longed to be in there, part of things, but I simply couldn't move. I didn't know what was the matter with me. I kept screwing myself up, teeth gritted, fists clenched, but my legs wouldn't move.

Then the art room door suddenly flew open and Daisy rushed out. She barged straight into me. 'What are you doing, hiding there?' she said, shaking her head at me.

I tried to relax my face, but not quickly enough.

'Have you got a pain?' Daisy asked.

I mumbled something vague.

'Is it your period?' Daisy said, sympathetic now.

I felt myself blushing. I knew it was silly, but we didn't even say the word at home. Mum had whispered some stuff about monthlies and bleeding and towels and then left me to get on with it. It was treated like a shameful secret. If Mum saw me rubbing my tummy or getting an aspirin she might whisper, 'Have you got your . . . ?' but she always let her voice tail away before uttering the taboo word. It was odd hearing Daisy discuss it so matter-of-factly.

'Shall I tell Rax you're not well?'

'*No!*' I said, dying at the thought of Daisy discussing my fictitious painful period with Mr Raxberry.

'Well, you'd better go and get cracking then. We're all doing a still life. I'm going to look for daisies for mine – like my name, get it? Rax says I won't be able to find any of them little white daisies but says there are these purply Michaelmas daisies, big ones, growing in the garden. He says no one will mind if I pick just one.'

Daisy hurried past me. I still stood there, motionless.

'Go *in* then, Prudence,' she said, turning. 'Don't look so scared. Rax won't get mad because you're late. He's dead cool, he never gets narked with anyone.'

I gave a little nod, took the deepest breath ever, and then went inside the art room. It seemed happily chaotic, students bobbing about in billowing smocks, setting up all sorts of still life arrangements, chatting to each other and calling to Mr Raxberry.

They were all calling him Rax to his face, but he didn't seem to mind. He strolled around, giving advice, juggling pots and books and ornaments into attractive still life arrangements, laughing as he listened to Rita going on about something.

He didn't have a clue I wasn't there. He couldn't care less.

I decided to slip straight out again while I had the chance. But as I turned he called my name.

'Prudence?'

I stopped, my heart thudding.

'Hi!' He came over to me. It was so strange seeing the real Mr Raxberry close up when I'd been imagining him so vividly. He was smiling at me, his eyes friendly, his head tilted slightly to one side, exactly the way I remembered.

'Did you get lost?'

'No. Well. Sort of,' I stammered idiotically.

'Don't worry. It took me weeks to find my way around. Tell you what, I'll draw you a little map.'

I thought he was joking and smiled.

'Now. We're setting up still life compositions, ones that hopefully reflect our personality, lifestyle, hobbies, whatever.' He looked at me. 'A still life is a fancy name for a lot of assorted objects. Look, here's some postcard reproductions.'

I shuffled them politely. I recognized most of them but held my tongue. I'd learned that some teachers thought you were showing off if you told them you knew all about something.

'Let's find you a little quiet spot in the midst of this bedlam.' He glanced round and saw an empty desk near Rita.

I couldn't bear the thought. 'How about over there?' I said quickly, nodding at the opposite corner where Sarah was happily splodging paint, her tongue sticking out with concentration.

'Great. Yes, keep Sarah company – but I think you'll need some kind of overall. Sarah gets a bit over-enthusiastic sometimes.'

'I haven't got one.' I looked down at my awful dress. 'I don't care if I get covered in paint, it won't matter in the slightest.'

Mr Raxberry raised his eyebrows but didn't argue. He found me paper, a couple of paintbrushes and six new pots of paint.

'OK, now it's down to you,' he said.

It was simple. I set up the paint pots, one paintbrush, the handful of postcards, and took *Jane Eyre* out of my school bag. I smoothed out my paper and started blocking in the shapes.

'You're doing that wrong,' said Daisy, bustling back with a handful of purple flowers. 'You paint *with* the paint pots, they're not supposed to go in the picture.'

'I *want* them to be part of my still life,' I said.

'But that's daft,' said Daisy.

'She's not daft, she's clever,' said Sarah. She smiled at me. 'We can do what we want. I'm painting red, lots and lots of red. I love red. I love your dress.'

'You're the only person in the whole world who loves this dress, but I'm glad you do,' I said. 'OK, I'll paint some red too. I'll paint the red paint pot first.'

'Nutters,' said Daisy, and barged past.

Sarah and I painted companionably. Sarah hummed tunelessly as she painted, but it was quite a soothing sound. I concentrated hard, so

106

so so wanting to impress Mr Raxberry. He was wandering round the classroom, talking, rearranging, suggesting, trying to get everyone to settle down.

He came over to Sarah, holding a Red Delicious apple, a chilli pepper and a crimson china teacup.

'Hey, more red things for you to paint. Let's mix up your palate and get lots of lovely different shades of red. A bit of yellow here – go on, splodge it around with your paintbrush, that's right. There, that's a perfect pepper colour.'

Sarah laughed delightedly. I loved the way he talked to her. Some of the teachers treated her like a baby, some of them simply ignored her, and some treated her warily, obviously uncomfortable. Mr Raxberry treated Sarah with gentle respect and she clearly adored him for it.

'I love you, Rax,' she said, when he let her take a bite of the red apple.

'You're a very sweet girl, Sarah,' he said. 'Don't take a bite of the pepper now, it'll be much too hot and you'll be in serious trouble with your teeth if you bite my china teacup.'

Sarah giggled at the joke. Then Mr Raxberry came over to me.

He stood silently, looking.

I sat silently, waiting.

My mouth dried. I could feel my heart thumping. It had been so horrible when hateful Mrs Godfrey had been scathing about my English essay, but I could bear that. I needed

Mr Raxberry to like my artwork. I needed it badly. I didn't dare look up to see the expression on his face.

Daisy was watching. 'She's done it wrong, hasn't she, Rax? You're not meant to paint the pots and brushes, you're meant to do your own still life, aren't you? Like me with my purple daisies.'

'No, she's got it absolutely spot on *right*,' said Mr Raxberry.

I breathed out.

'You and your Michaelmas daisies are right for you, Daisy. Prudence feels that art materials and books are right for her.'

'Boring,' said Daisy, pulling a face.

I swallowed. 'So it's OK?' I whispered, still not looking up.

'You know it is,' said Mr Raxberry. He paused. Then he said softly, 'You're going to be the girl that makes my teaching worthwhile.'

I started to get into this new strange routine. I
went to school, I stumbled through the fog of
lessons, I went to Mr Raxberry's art class and
the sun shone, dazzling me, and then I went to
the stroke unit every evening and endured
thunderstorms with Dad.

It was so unfair. I had to do all the talking to
him. Mum contented herself sorting Dad's
laundry and trying to feed him sloppy snacks –
yoghurt and ice cream and cold rice pudding –
though his false teeth were now firmly back in
place and all too snappy.

Grace pressed herself right against the wall of
his room, as if trying to burrow right through it
into the toilet next door. She said nothing at all
unless directly questioned. Sometimes her hands
did tiny Iggy-Figgy-Piggy waves to herself.

I was the one who had to be the teacher for an hour or more, after a long day at school forced to be a pupil. I couldn't prepare what I was going to do because it so much depended on Dad's mood. I tried drawing a whole series of everyday objects familiar to him: a shelf of books, a shirt, trousers, a cup of tea, a plate of fish and chips, with the word carefully printed underneath. The first time I produced them Dad was tired after a tussle with the physiotherapist. He barely glanced at each card and shook his head lethargically whenever I asked him to say a word.

'Poor dear, he's not up to it,' Mum murmured.

I felt Dad simply couldn't be bothered. I was tempted to draw pink and black lace underwear to see if that got any response.

I tried again the next evening and this time Dad *over*reacted. When I showed him the cards his good hand whipped out and smacked them away.

'Damn-fool, damn-fool, damn-fool,' he growled. 'Not blooming *baby*.'

At least he was saying words, even though they were unprompted ones. I gave up the cards after that, although lovely Nurse Ray collected them up and asked if she could use them for some of her other patients.

I was so pleased I did her a set for all the old lady stroke victims, drawing a lipstick, a hairbrush, a nightie, a photo of grandchildren and a television. The nurse gave me a kiss and said I was an inventive little angel.

I decided I wouldn't bother trying to teach Dad any more. It was clearly a waste of time.

The next visit Dad was lying prone on his pillows, grey with fatigue, purple circles under his eyes. I thought he'd be extra irritable, but he grabbed hold of my wrist and tears ran down his face, dribbling sideways into his ears. I didn't know if his eyes were watering from exhaustion or whether he was really crying. I felt awkward and embarrassed, but tender too. I sat down beside him on the edge of his bed, trying to reassure him that he'd soon get better, he'd be out of hospital right as rain, ready to teach us and take us out on trips. I reminded him of all the places we'd visited, and Dad made a stab at repeating 'National Gallery', 'Hampton Court', 'Windsor Castle', 'Box Hill' and 'Hastings'. Most of the words sounded weird, but when prompted he could tell me which one had paintings, which was once owned by a Tudor king, which was owned by our current Queen, which was a high hill with a perilous chalk path and which was famous for a long-ago battle.

It was hard putting all this effort into teaching Dad, and then having to go home and do my own homework. I learned which teachers would simply moan a bit but not pursue it if you failed to hand it in, and which would harass and hound you. Mrs Godfrey was Queen Harasser and Hounder. I drew a picture of her like a one-breasted Amazon driving her wheel-spiked chariot while bloodied pupils wailed in her wake.

I didn't have an Iggy-Figgy back-up system like Grace. I had to ~~struggle by myself.~~ Sometimes the English homework seemed ridiculously easy, and the French and history and religious education and PSHE seemed a total doddle most of the time, but I floundered hopelessly with the science and ICT and maths. I *wished* we got art homework. I only had two double lessons of art each week, nowhere near enough.

I worked hard on my still life. I added a few extra favourite books – *The Bell Jar*, *The Catcher in the Rye*, *Tess of the D'Urbervilles*, *Frankenstein* and *The Chrysalids*, shamelessly trying to impress Mr Raxberry.

He nodded at each title, giving me his little smile. 'Mrs Godfrey would be proud of you,' he said.

'Mrs Godfrey *hates* me,' I said.

'No she doesn't!'

'She does, she finds me fantastically irritating. She's forever putting me down and punishing me. I don't know why, because I try really hard in English. Well, I did. I can't be bothered now.'

'Keep bothering, Prue. Maybe you disconcert her. She's not used to girls like you.'

'I'm not used to women like her,' I said. I paused. 'I wish all the teachers were like you, Mr Raxberry.'

'Shameless flattery will probably make you teacher's pet,' he said, laughing. Then he looked at me more seriously. 'Are you finding it all a bit of a struggle?'

'A bit,' I said carefully. Understatement of the century!

'And someone in the staff room said your dad's not well at the moment?'

'He's had a stroke. He's getting a bit better now, but still can't move much, or say many words.' My voice went wobbly as I said it.

Mr Raxberry looked at me, his eyes warm and concerned. 'It must be horrible for you,' he said. 'If it gets too much any time, use the art room as a bolt hole. Painting is excellent therapy. Here, this should help you find your way around.'

He tucked a roll of paper into my school bag. I didn't look at it there and then in front of everyone. I waited until I got home, and Grace was in the kitchen having a snack with Mum. The rolled-up paper was fastened with scarlet ribbon. I untied it, smoothed it out against my hot cheek, and then wound it round my finger like a fat silk ring. Then I carefully smoothed out the long rectangle of paper.

It was the map he'd promised me. He'd drawn the school in three dimensions, with the appropriate teacher in their classroom – each a wicked caricature. He'd drawn strange alien creatures lurking in the cloakroom and gnawing pizzas in the canteen. A great tribe of these two-headed claw-footed horned and tailed beings ran amok in the playground. He'd drawn me cowering away from them in my red-and-white

113

tablecloth dress. I was standing at the start of a tiny scarlet pathway. I followed it with my finger, all the way past the playing fields, straight to the art block, where Mr Raxberry was painting at an easel.

I kissed the tip of my finger and then very carefully pressed it down on the tiny figure.

I didn't take my map back to school. I looked at it so often I could still see it written in the air after I'd rolled it up. I tucked it carefully in my drawer with the underwear set I never wanted to wear again.

Oh God, that underwear! The girls must have told the boys. They all seemed incredibly interested in it.

'Come on, Prue, show us your slaggy underwear,' they yelled after me.

They crept up behind me and pinged the elastic of my bra through my dress and tried to pull up my skirt. I hated the feel of their hot scrabbly hands. I knew I should stay calm and disdainful, but I shrieked and slapped at them, making a spectacle of myself. Then they'd mimic me and say stupid things until I was nearly in tears. Rita and her little gang, Aimee, Megan and Jess, would watch, smiling.

Mr Raxberry came along the corridor in the midst of one of these episodes.

'Hey, guys, make room for a member of the hallowed staff,' he said, waving them out the way.

They sauntered off, not too bothered whether he'd seen or not, because he was only old Rax.

114

Mr Raxberry paused, pretending to be looking at messages on the notice board. His back was to me, but when I started creeping away he turned and came over. 'Were they giving you a hard time?' he said.

'No, no!' I said, scarlet.

I couldn't bear the idea of telling him, maybe having to bring my underwear into the conversation. Mr Raxberry knew I was lying, of course, but he simply nodded. He walked along the corridor beside me, changing the subject, talking about an arts programme that evening.

'It's on cable telly. Do you get it? If not, I could maybe video it for you,' he suggested.

'That's very kind, Mr Raxberry, but actually. I don't have any kind of television, or a video either,' I said.

I waited for him to shake his head in astonishment and act like I was a creature from a different planet, but he just nodded again.

'So that's how you find the time to read so much,' he said. 'I should get rid of our television. My little boy watches endless horrible cartoons. I'm sure it's not good for him. Maybe that's why he keeps trying to beat up his baby sister.'

'You've got children,' I said. My voice sounded odd. I felt as if someone was squeezing my throat. It was such a shock. I knew he was probably in his mid-twenties, plenty old enough to have children. I knew he probably had a partner. Well . . . I hadn't actually thought about it too much. He was Mr Raxberry, my art teacher, not Mr

Raxberry, family man, with wife and two kids.

'My little boy's three. He's called Harry. And Lily's six months old. Hang on.' He felt in the back pocket of his jeans for his wallet. 'Here they are,' he said, showing me a photo.

I looked at the dark little boy clasping a roly-poly baby a little too tightly. They seemed surprisingly uninteresting, nondescript children, nothing like their father.

'They're lovely.' I tried to sound enthusiastic. I wondered what his wife looked like. Did I dare ask? 'Do you have a photo of your wife too?'

He paused a moment. 'Yes. Yes, there's one of all of us in here *somewhere*.' He fumbled amongst five-pound notes and travel cards and bunched-up stamps, and eventually found a crumpled holiday snapshot.

It was of the whole family, walking along an esplanade, squinting in the strong sunshine. Mr Raxberry was in denim shorts, a black sleeveless T-shirt and canvas shoes. He looked less like a teacher than ever. He was pushing a little baby Lily in a buggy. Her sunhat had fallen sideways, almost totally obscuring her face, but she was kicking her fat little legs contentedly. The little boy was scowling under his baseball cap, hanging on to his mother's hand, looking as if he was whining to be carried.

I looked at her. She wasn't as pretty as I'd thought she'd be. She was wearing shorts too, baggy ones down to her knees, with a big T-shirt over the top. She was obviously self-conscious about her figure. She wasn't fat, not like Grace, certainly not like poor Mum, but she was a little too curvy, big breasts but also a big tummy and a big bottom. Maybe she simply hadn't got her figure back after having the baby.

I looked at her face. It was difficult to tell what she was really like because she was frowning in the sunlight. The little boy was pestering her too. She wouldn't look happy and relaxed in these circumstances. Her hair was lovely though, soft and shining and fair, in a pageboy bob just brushing her shoulders. So Mr Raxberry liked big, curvy blondes. I wished I wasn't small and thin and dark.

I tried hard to think of something to say. There were a hundred questions I wanted to ask. Why *her* out of all the hundreds of women you must have met? What makes her so special? Do you tell her all your secrets? Does she put her arms round you and soothe you when you're tired or worried? Does she paint too? Does she read? Do you both sketch on holiday and then sit cosily at either end of the sofa, toes touching, reading your books? Do you go shopping together? Do you have the children in bed for a big family cuddle on Sunday mornings? Is she your childhood sweetheart, your one true love?

'What's her name?' I asked out loud.

'Marianne.'

'Oh. That's nice,' I said lamely. 'I wish I had a pretty name like that.'

'What's wrong with Prudence?'

117

'What's *right* with it? It's an awful Victorian virtue name. My dad used to be very religious. He really went overboard. I'm Prudence Charity and my sister's Grace Patience, can you believe it?'

'I've got a terrible name too. Keith. How naff is that, especially as I used to have a bit of a lisp as a child. Imagine! "My name's Keef." Thank God most people called me Rax. No, you're lucky, Prudence and Grace are quaintly beautiful names. They make me think of little Victorian girls in pinafores and button boots.'

'Exactly,' I said. 'My clothes are almost as old-fashioned!'

I was still rotating my hideous dresses. Mum had sent me to school with ten pounds. She thought we could be kitted out in second-hand uniform for a fiver each. But the school shop didn't charge jumble-sale prices. Each garment cost a fortune, even the old threadbare stuff. I bought us a shabby blazer which we wore in turns. It was too tight for Grace and it absolutely swamped me, but I was past caring.

Mum was appalled that it was going to be so expensive acquiring a whole uniform. She did question me several times on the exact price of the blouses and skirts and school ties. I heard her asking Grace too, as if she didn't believe me. I suppose she felt she couldn't trust me after I'd spent the maths tuition money.

'I think your clothes kind of suit you, Prudence,' said Mr Raxberry.

'I hate them,' I said. 'I can't wait to get the proper school uniform, but it's going to take ages before we can afford it all.'

Mr Raxberry paused. 'Perhaps . . . perhaps you could earn a bit yourself?'

'I don't know how. I can't get a Saturday job because I have to help in our bookshop and I don't get paid for that. I'd do a paper round but the shop down our street doesn't do deliveries any more. I can't think of anything else I could do.'

'Babysitting?'

'I don't know anyone with babies.'

'You know me,' said Mr Raxberry.

I stared at him. 'Do you really mean it?'

'Why not? Marianne and I need to get out more. I don't think we've had one proper evening out since Lily was born. How about it? Maybe Friday? Say seven thirty? We'll be back by eleven and I'll drive you home of course. Do you think your mother would mind?'

'Of course she won't mind!' I said.

Mum *did* mind, terribly.

'What do you *mean*, this teacher has asked you to babysit, Prudence? He barely knows you. You've only been at the school five minutes.'

It felt as if I'd known Mr Raxberry all my life, but I knew it might not be wise to say this to Mum.

'It's Mr Raxberry, Mum,' I said.

'Oh, Rax,' said Grace.

She called him by his nickname, even though he didn't even teach her year. I'd never been able to psych myself up to calling him Rax. It seemed too intimate and personal, even though the whole school, teachers, pupils, even the dinner ladies, called him Rax too.

'I don't care who he is, you're not going to a strange man's house,' said Mum.

'He's *not* a strange man, Mum. You've met him, remember? The teacher with the little beard and the earring.'

'Oh. Him! So he's got a *baby*? He didn't look old enough.'

'He's got a little boy, Harry, and a baby, Lily. And I'm babysitting for them on Friday night.'

'You are *lucky*, Prue. Can I come too?' Grace begged.

'No, it's just me. It will look as if we're asking for double the money if you come too, Grace,' I said quickly. 'He only asked me because I was moaning about not being able to afford the school uniform.'

I didn't want Grace tagging along too. I wanted to keep Mr Raxberry and his family all to myself.

'How dare you tell a teacher we can't afford the uniform!' said Mum.

'But it's true, we can't.'

'That's *our* business. You shouldn't go round blabbing about our finances,' said Mum, red with mortification.

'I don't *blab*,' I said. 'This was a private

120

conversation with my art teacher. And do you have any idea how awful it is to be the only girl in the school – well, apart from Grace – not to be wearing a proper uniform? I can't stand wearing this awful dress—'

Grace gasped. Mum looked stricken. I had always pretended I liked my terrible outfits so as not to hurt Mum's feelings. But what about *my* feelings?

'I'm sorry, I don't want to be rude—'

'Then *don't*,' said Grace.

'But it *is* awful, having to wear little girly dresses. They were fine when we were small, Mum, but now we just look eccentric and old-fashioned.'

'Well, I can't kit you out in a whole new set of clothing just because you feel embarrassed to be wearing my home-made clothes,' Mum said. She tried to sound cool and dignified, but there were tears in her eyes.

'I know, I know. That's why I want to earn some money babysitting,' I persisted.

'You don't know anything about babies.'

'It's not a *tiny* baby. She's sitting up, probably crawling around. And the little boy's three going on four. Anyway, they'll be in *bed*. All I have to do is be there, just in case they wake up and want a drink or whatever.'

'You might have to change a nappy,' said Grace. 'You won't like that. You practically throw up if you step in dog poo.'

'Shut up!' I said, my stomach heaving. I'd even

manage dirty nappies if it meant being at Mr Raxberry's house.

'How will you get home?' said Mum. 'I'm not having you walking the streets at night, but we can't afford a taxi.'

'Mr Raxberry is going to drive me home.' I said it calmly, though my blood fizzed at the thought. Mr Raxberry and me, alone in the car, driving home in the dark . . .

'I still don't like the idea. And goodness knows what your dad will say,' said Mum. She suddenly nodded triumphantly. 'What are we thinking of? You can't go, Prue, you'll be visiting your father at the hospital.'

'I can take one evening off,' I said. 'Just *one*.'

'He'll wonder where you are.'

'You can tell him I'm babysitting.'

'I can't say it's for your *teacher*. Your dad will have another stroke if he knows you're going to school.'

'He'll have to know *some*time, Mum.'

'I know, I know. But not yet, when he's still so poorly,' she said.

'Well, I'm still going babysitting on Friday, Mum, no matter what you say. I'll see Dad tonight; I'll see him every single night except Friday.'

'He'll fret about it.'

'I can't help it. I'm the one who has to sort him out and teach him and go over stuff. It's OK for you and Grace, you just sit there.'

'I know, dear. I'd be happy to take my turn,

but I just don't seem to have the knack for it.'

'I *certainly* don't,' said Grace.

'It's so hard, and I keep getting behind with my homework and getting into trouble at school,' I whined.

'You could try explaining that you're having to help out with your dad,' said Mum guiltily.

'I don't want to talk to them about Dad,' I said, sensing Mum was weakening. 'I just want to help out, Mum. I want to help Dad. I want to earn a bit of spare money. I know we're horribly in debt, I've seen all the bills.' I paused. 'I feel especially bad about that sixty pounds. I just didn't realize. I'd take the underwear back but I've already worn it. I've *got* to earn it back, then I won't feel quite so bad.'

'Oh lovie, all right, all right. I understand,' said Mum, patting my shoulder.

Grace understood more fully. She waited until we were in bed.

'What's this thing with old Rax, Prue?' she whispered. 'Why do you really want to babysit?'

'I *said*, I want to earn some money.'

'Yeah, but you're so *keen*.' She thought about it. 'Are you keen on *Rax*, Prue?'

'Of course not,' I said hurriedly.

'You're always hanging round the art block. And you always go pink when he says hello to you.'

'I do not!'

'Yes you do. Yeah, you've got a thing about him, haven't you?'

'No, I haven't. For goodness' sake, he's a boring old *teacher*.'

'Yes, but he's not really like the others. He's much more laid back and casual. Of course he's not really good looking—'

'Yes he is!' I said.

'What, with that weird little beard? Iggy and Figgy and me think beards are so gross. And then he's got this earring. Iggy says it means you're gay if you just wear one earring, though I suppose he can't be if he's got a wife and two children.'

'I don't care if he's got a boyfriend, a girlfriend, or a beard like Father Christmas. I just want to do some babysitting to earn a bit of extra cash, that's all,' I declared. 'Now shut up and go to sleep.'

She did shut up. I thought I had her convinced. But later, when she turned over, she mumbled, 'You *do* so fancy him. You can't fool me, Prudence King.'

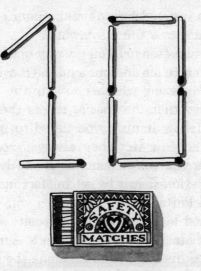

I told Mr Raxberry I could babysit on Friday. I announced it as casually as I could, leaving it right to the end of the art lesson, acting like I'd almost forgotten about it.

'Oh, thanks,' he said, equally casual, as if it was the most ordinary everyday thing in the world. Maybe it was. Maybe half the class already babysat for the Raxberry household.

He told me his address and told me his road was on the number 37 bus route.

'Fine, no problem,' I said.

I wondered if he expected me to bus home after all? He *had* said he'd drive me home, hadn't he? Or had I just made that bit up? I couldn't help imagining Mr Raxberry in my head, the way I'd always imagined Jane and Tobias – but I didn't get muddled with them, because they weren't real.

Tobias insisted he *was* real, materializing as I walked across the playground.

I was supposed to be on my way to the Success Maker centre for an hour's maths coaching, but I was wondering whether to skip the class. I'd discovered that the special tutors there didn't always follow it up if you failed to put in an appearance. In fact they always greeted you with extreme enthusiasm, as if you'd passed a difficult exam simply by setting foot inside their glorified Portakabin.

I looked longingly in the opposite direction, towards Mr Raxberry's art block. I imagined myself on his map, running along the little red road.

'You can't go there. He's busy teaching,' said Tobias, pulling me back. 'Talk to *me*. We haven't spent any time together for ages. Please, Prue.'

'Oh go away. I'm not in the mood,' I muttered.

'You be careful. If you keep ignoring me I'll go away altogether, and then where will you be when you're lonely?' said Tobias. 'Watch out. I'm fading a little already.'

I looked at him. His beautiful face was blurred, his golden curls tarnishing to fawn, his blue eyes barely there.

I felt a pang, knowing that he was right. All my imaginary friends had faded away as I'd gradually grown out of them. I could barely remember the strange companions of my little girlhood: the white rabbit as tall as my waist, the flock of flower fairies, the tame green dragon with crimson claws, the black and white jumping cow who flew me over the moon . . .

Even Jane was fading now, though she had been my constant friend for years. I tried to conjure her up in a panic, but she pressed herself against the corridor walls, her back to me, refusing to show me her face.

'You see,' said Tobias. 'Watch out, Prue, or you'll lose me too. I'll go for good, I'm warning you.'

His attitude was starting to irritate me. He was a figment of my imagination. What made him think he could threaten me like this?

'Go then,' I said rashly. 'See if I care. I can always make someone else up.'

I turned away from him – and the Success Maker. I started marching back across the playground. I decided to hide in the girls' cloakrooms until the bell went. I had a book in my school bag. I'd be fine. I didn't need Tobias.

'Hey, Prue,' he called after me.

I heard him running – and then he caught hold of me. His hand was on my shoulder, clutching it. I turned. There he was, his fair hair tousled, a smile on his face, a real boy, so real I could see the freckles on his nose, smell his shampoo, feel the warmth of his body.

'Tobias!' I blurted, like an idiot.

'Tobias? No, I'm Toby,' he said.

Of course it was only that Toby from my class, Rita's boyfriend, the one most of the girls fancied.

'Oh, sorry,' I mumbled.

'Tobias!' he said, in a pseudo-posh voice, mocking me.

'Yeah, right, I know,' I said. I tried to act cool and casual, but sounded like a sad member of the Iggy-Figgy-Piggy club.

'You're going the wrong way,' he said. 'The Success Maker's that way.' He gestured over his shoulder.

'Yes, I know.'

'Aren't you supposed to be going for the maths session?'

'I don't feel like it right now, OK?'

He raised his eyebrows. 'Can't say I blame you. I've just been for an English session and it's doing my head in. Tell you what, let's skip everything and go for a smoke.'

I stared at him. I didn't want to go with him at all. I wasn't even sure what 'going for a smoke' really meant. Was it some sort of euphemism? But Rita had been particularly mean to me that morning, making stupid remarks, and when I'd tried to ignore her by reading my book she'd snatched it from me and thrown it in a corner, tearing the dust wrapper and crumpling several pages. I'd felt like slapping her, but she was bigger than me, and Aimee and Megan and Jess would start on me too. Going for a smoke with Rita's precious boyfriend seemed an easier way of getting my revenge.

'Sure,' I said. 'So. Where are your cigarettes, then?'

'Not *here*. Behind the bike sheds,' Toby hissed.

In every school story I'd ever read the rebellious children got up to mischief *behind the bike sheds*. I looked at him sharply, wondering if this was some elaborate wind-up. He was certainly behaving theatrically, putting his finger to his lips as we walked stealthily past the classroom windows.

I followed him, walking normally. I hummed under my breath to show him he couldn't boss me about. He shook his head at me, but waited until we were away from the classrooms, approaching these infamous bike sheds. I thought he'd tell me off, but he seemed impressed.

'You are so cool, Prue. You just don't care, do you?'

I shrugged.

'Is that why you're here? Did you get expelled from your old school?'

'I've not been to school, not for years. I went when I was little, but then my dad kept me and my sister at home.'

I peered at all the bikes in the banal little shed. It didn't really seem like a Den of Iniquity. Toby leaned against the ripples of the corrugated iron wall and fished a squashed packet of cigarettes and a box of matches out of his back pocket. I felt hugely relieved.

I'd never smoked before and inhaled warily when he lit one for me.

'You smoke then?' Toby said.

'Yeah,' I said, blinking because my eyes were

starting to water. I held my chest muscles rigid, determined not to cough.

'Rita's always nagging me to give up,' said Toby.

'Well. Rita's always nagging, full stop,' I said.

'Yeah, I can't stick that in a girl. They go on about how they're mad about you and then they end up mad *with* you, bossing you about all the time, trying to get you to change.' He paused. 'Have you got a boyfriend, Prue?'

I felt my face getting hot.

'You're blushing! Come on, who is he?'

'There's no one, really.'

'Yes there is!'

'No. Well, there's someone I *like*.'

'Ah!' said Toby. He inhaled deeply and then blew expert smoke rings.

I tried to copy but couldn't quite get the hang of it, though he did his best to show me how to shape my lips and tongue. I started feeling dizzy from inhaling. I leaned back against the wall myself, shutting my eyes for a second.

When I opened them Toby's face was alarmingly close to mine, making me start. His eyes were half-closed, his lips puckered, almost as if he was about to kiss me.

I moved sideways sharply.

'Hey, don't run away,' he said. He reached out for me but I ducked away.

'Prue, come on. I'm just trying to be friendly.'

'Yeah. And what would Rita have to say about that?'

'Rita doesn't own me. Sometimes I wonder what I ever saw in her.'

'Oh come on, she's the prettiest girl in the class.'

'You're prettier than she is. Listen, I've been thinking. You're not so great at maths and IT, right?'

'That's putting it mildly.'

'Well, I'm a whiz at it, honest. It's just I'm rubbish at reading.'

'What, you don't like it?'

'I can't *do* it,' said Toby, shuffling. 'It's not that I'm *thick*. I'm severely dyslexic – that's what they say.'

'You mean you can't read at all?' I said, wondering how he could bear a world where books were meaningless.

'Yeah, I can *read*,' he said, flushing. 'I know all the words and stuff, it's just that I get them all mixed up. Plus at my old school they used to make fun of me, so I just stopped trying and messed around. *Anyway*, what I was thinking, you're obviously the hotshot at English. You talk like you've swallowed the dictionary and you can run rings round Mrs Godfrey, so how about you giving me a bit of extra coaching? Then I can help you with maths and IT in return. OK?'

'I don't know.' I stubbed out my cigarette, thinking about it. 'When would we do this coaching?'

'We could get together at lunch time.'

'Oh yes, Rita will be thrilled.'

'I told you, Rita doesn't own me. I'm sick of her telling me what to do.' He was obviously worrying about it all the same. 'Tell you what!' he said, smiling. 'We could go round each other's houses once or twice a week. What are you doing tonight after school?'

'I've got to go and visit my dad in hospital.'

'Well, tomorrow then. Friday?'

'Not Friday. I definitely can't make Friday.'

'Why? What are you doing then? Seeing your boyfriend?'

'I *said*, I don't have one. No, I'm babysitting.'

'Oh, right.' He didn't pursue it. He offered me another cigarette. I refused, feeling dizzy enough with just one. He edged up close again, so I started walking away smartly.

'Hey, come back. You can't just stalk off like that – someone will see you're not in class.'

'I don't care.'

'You really don't, do you?' he said. 'You're so different from all the other girls, Prue.'

'I wish I wasn't.'

'Are they giving you a hard time?' he asked. 'You come and tell me if they get at you too much. I'll sort them out for you.'

'Yeah, they'll relish that,' I said sarcastically.

'So, when are we going to get it together for these coaching sessions?'

'Sometime,' I said. I wouldn't commit myself any more.

'And are you going to give me a kiss sometime soon?' he asked.

'This year, next year, *sometime* . . . or maybe never,' I said, running off.

He ran after me, trying to grab hold of my hand, but I kept snatching it away. We must have run past Grace's class because she was all agog when we went home from school.

'You were holding hands with Toby Baker!' she said.

'How do you know Toby Baker?'

'*Everyone* knows him. Iggy and Figgy think he's dead cool.'

'Well, they're easily impressed. And I wasn't holding hands with him. I wouldn't.'

'*I* would,' said Grace. 'He's just, like, drop-dead gorgeous.'

I sighed at her. 'Shut up! You sound so vacant. You don't really think that at all – you don't like boys any more than I do. You're just saying stuff to impress Iggy and Figgy but they're not here, right, it's just you and me, so stop *pretending*.'

Grace blinked at me, looking wounded. 'I thought you were all in *favour* of pretending,' she said. 'Why do you have to be so horrid about Iggy and Figgy, they're my *friends*. I'm not talking to you now, see!'

I laughed at her. I knew Grace couldn't keep quiet for more than five minutes. Only *one* minute later she said, 'What were you doing with Toby Baker anyway? Is he your boyfriend?'

'No. Though I think he'd like it if he was. He kept pestering me,' I said.

I wasn't interested in Toby, but I couldn't help

enjoying the fact that he liked me, especially as so many girls seemed crazy about him. I knew he was the golden boy of our class, but I hadn't realized he was an icon throughout the school, with worshippers as small and silly as Iggy and Figgy.

'I wish you would go out with him. Iggy and Figgy would be seriously impressed if they knew Toby Baker was going out with my sister. Then you could invite him round to tea and I could invite them and they could actually meet him.'

'He wants to come round to our place so we can help each other with stuff.'

'Oh Prue!' Grace started skipping, her pink panda dress wafting alarmingly high up her large legs.

'For heaven's sake, Grace, stop acting like a toddler.'

'Don't be mean again.'

'Well, don't be so babyish. And there's no need to get excited anyway – I'm not having him round.'

'Oh!'

'Can you just imagine it, with Mum flapping round and asking him all sorts?'

'Yes, I suppose. And Dad would go bonkers if he found out you had a boyfriend.'

'Dad *is* bonkers now,' I said, sighing.

I didn't really mean it. I knew my father wasn't intellectually impaired. But he couldn't help sounding weird as he parroted key words and phrases after me. He sounded demented whenever he threw a tantrum and repeated the same swearword over and over again, like a satanic version of a Buddhist chant.

He was in a foul mood that night because the physiotherapist had made him wear someone else's shorts for his exercise session. Dad was outraged, utterly refusing to co-operate, hissing with rage whenever he looked down at his sad, skinny legs. He'd always loathed shorts on anyone, male or female. Grace and I weren't even allowed to wear them as little girls.

Mum helped him into his pyjamas while we lurked outside his room, but Dad stayed infuriated, even decently covered in his blue and white stripes. He kept pointing at the baggy black shorts hanging from the end of his bed. He acted as if a giant black bat was flapping from his bedpost.

'Yes, Dad. Shorts,' I said meanly. 'Say the word "shorts".'

Dad said a much more graphic word.

'They just want to help you, Bernard,' Mum said. 'The physiotherapist says she's sure you could get the use of your leg back if you'd just try to co-operate.'

'I know you don't like doing the exercises, Dad, but they're good for you,' I said.

'I hate exercises too. PE's my worst thing at school,' said Grace.

There was a sudden silence. Grace sat very still, her eyes bulging as she realized what she'd said. Mum looked agonized. Dad shook his head irritably.

'What?' he said. 'What? *What?*'

'She said she hated exercise, dear. So do I. Now, where's the girl gone with the tea trolley? Isn't it time you had a nice cup of tea?'

Dad looked at her scornfully. He could see through her diversionary tactics in two seconds. He turned to me. 'What?' he repeated.

'Grace and I have started a school game, Dad,' I said. 'We're teaching each other, setting each other tasks, as you're ill and can't do it for us just at the moment. The rule is, we have to do absolutely everything the other one asks. So I get a bit mean to poor Gracie sometimes, and make her do all these exercises for PE.'

Dad's eyes were narrowed. I stared innocently back at him. Then he suddenly started laughing, wheezing away as if he was about to break in two.

'*More* PE. More more more. Grace fat!'

I forced myself to laugh too. Mum laughed. Grace laughed the loudest.

It was OK. We'd got away with it.

I walked along Laurel Grove, peering at all the neat 1930s houses. I looked at the bay trees in ornamental blue pots outside front doors, the carriage lamps, the pebbles and spiky plants in mock Japanese gardens. I couldn't imagine Mr Raxberry living there. Surely anyone with an earring and artistic tendencies would be considered deeply suspect?

I checked the address, written in his own lovely italic writing on the back of my school jotter in my bag, though I knew I'd got it right. My bag was full of things to do: my sketchpad and crayons, patchwork, two novels and an old shop copy of Penelope Leach's baby book in case of emergencies.

Number 28, 30, 32 – and there was number 34 Laurel Grove. At first glance it didn't look any different from the other houses in the road, a black and white semi-detached house with a sloping roof and a green front door. At *second* glance, as I walked up the garden path, it stayed an ordinary, slightly shabby house with an abandoned Thomas the Tank Engine shunted into a cotoneaster bush and muddy frog wellingtons lolling on the porch. Mr Raxberry didn't belong here. He should be living in an urban warehouse flat, large and airy and white, with huge canvases on the wall and a large easel in the centre of the room. I saw him there, painting, his face tense with concentration, his earring catching the sunlight. I was sitting on a black leather sofa, talking to him while he painted my portrait. *That's* the way it should be.

I rang the doorbell and waited. I could see into the living room, glimpse the cream canvas chairs and the beige sofa and the bleak square shelving. I *must* have come to the wrong address.

Then the door opened. There was Mr Raxberry in black jeans, soft blue shirt and bare feet, but he was holding a baby, a little girl with tufty black hair and a cross expression. She was wearing a small navy jumper and nothing else. Her little pink bottom perched neatly on Mr Raxberry's hand.

'Hi, Prue. Sorry, we're in the middle of a nappy change, aren't we, Lily?'

Lily grizzled irritably. I held out my hand to her uncertainly and she reared away from me, butting her head against Mr Raxberry's shoulder. She started crying in earnest.

'Take no notice, she's tired,' said Mr Raxberry. 'Come in, come in.'

I stepped into the hall and followed him towards the beige living room. The carpet was strewn with wooden blocks and wax crayons and limp teddy bears.

'Sorry! We'll get cleared up in a jiffy. I'll just shove a nappy on Lily. Marianne's upstairs giving Harry his bath. She'll be down in a minute. Would you like a coffee or a Coke or something? And I'd better show you how the television works.' He said all this boring ordinary stuff, the baby still balanced in his hand, but his eyes were looking at me. *They* were saying, 'Hark at me, bleating all this suburban daddy stuff. What am I *like*?'

'It's OK,' I said. 'I'll clear up the living room if you want to go and do the baby.' I wondered if I ought to fix the nappy myself but I didn't want him to see me struggling, doubtless snapping the wrong bits together.

He smiled at me gratefully and went upstairs with his grizzly little girl. I got down on my hands and knees and started gathering toys. The carpet was a bit gritty and could have done with a good going over with a hoover. Mum would have been ashamed to have a visitor see her house in such a state. Maybe Mrs Raxberry simply couldn't be bothered? I imagined her sprawling on the sofa, stuffing chocolates and watching television while the baby wailed and the little boy created havoc.

Why would Mr Raxberry want a wife like that? Why didn't he want a wife who was artistic and creative? He was so chic and stylish himself. Why not go for a complementary partner?

Mrs Raxberry came into the room at that moment. I stared at her, startled. I'd been imagining her as this great wobbly jelly woman when she was just an ordinary fair-haired mum, thinner now than the photo in his wallet, though the woollen dress she was wearing was clinging a little too closely.

'Hello! You must be Prudence. I'm Marianne. Oh God, I'm sorry, let me do that. I meant to get everything cleared up before you came but it's just been one of those days, and the kids have been driving me crazy.'

I must have looked alarmed. She laughed at me. 'Don't worry, they'll be fine. They'll both sleep like logs now. Harry's putting up a *bit* of a fight about going to bed, but it's not like it's a major strop.'

With perfect timing Harry started screaming upstairs: 'Mum! You come back now! I need you *now*! I want a story NOW!'

Mrs Raxberry raised her eyebrows and sighed. 'Can't you see to him, Keith?' she called up the stairs. She turned to me. 'Harry's a bit unsettled because we haven't been out for ages. He'll calm down soon, I promise. Keith will just read him one more story so he doesn't get too worked up, and then I'm sure he'll drop off. If he gets *really* upset, though, you can always ring us at the restaurant, I've left my mobile number by the telephone. I don't really know why we're going out for a meal. I had some fish fingers with Harry at tea time to keep him company even though I'm supposed to be on a diet. Does this dress look much too tight still? It looks really awful, doesn't it?'

'No, no, it looks lovely on you,' I lied.

I was disarmed by the way she talked to me like a friend she'd known for years. I didn't want to be her friend. I didn't want her to be so nice.

She wasn't so nice to Mr Raxberry though. Harry was still shrieking.

'For God's *sake*, Keith, can't you read Harry his story?'

'I'm changing Lily's nappy at this exact moment in time,' he called back.

'Can't you do both? Haven't you heard of multi-tasking?' She sighed, raising her eyebrows at me. 'Men! Why do they have to make changing a nappy into such a big deal? It's like he wants a medal pinned to his chest every time he does it.'

I wriggled uncomfortably, not knowing what to say.

'Oops! I keep forgetting he's your teacher. What's he like at school, eh? Is he pretty hopeless?'

'He's a brilliant teacher,' I said stiffly. 'He's taught me so much already.'

'Yes, I know you like art. Keith's told me all about you.'

I wanted to ask exactly what he'd said, getting her to repeat it word for word, but I was too shy.

'Art's my favourite subject,' I said. 'I want to go to art school.'

'Ah. Well, try not to end up an art teacher, Prudence.'

I made some non-committal noise. She was standing on tiptoe, peering at herself in the mirror above the mantelpiece.

'This dress *is* too tight, especially if I'm going to be having a big meal. I wanted to go to see a film tonight but there doesn't seem to be much on. I think I'll change into my navy top and my white trousers, yeah?' She looked at me. 'You're so lucky to be so skinny. Mind you, I wasn't much bigger than you before I had Harry. Dire warning: don't have kids! Come on, you'd better come and meet them. You can get them sorted out while I change. Keith's probably put a nappy on Harry and is reading *The Gruffalo* to Lily.'

I found Mr Raxberry sitting up on Harry's bed, with Lily on his lap and Harry cuddled against his chest. Lily was still nappyless. Harry was muttering in an ungrateful monotone, 'Don't want you reading, Daddy, I want *Mum*.'

I decided I didn't much care for either child. Harry was one of those bullet-headed little boys, wriggling and squirming and grumbling. Lily seemed sweeter, but her pink prawn limbs and bare bottom made me feel a bit squeamish. I put on a false smile nevertheless.

'What lovely children,' I said, practically clapping my hands and applauding them.

'Who's that big girl? I don't like her,' said Harry.

'That's Prudence. She's going to look after you and Lily tonight,' said Mr Raxberry.

I knew this was a silly thing to say. Harry reacted predictably, insisting he didn't want to be looked after by me, he didn't like me, he didn't like his dad either, he wanted *Mum*. Mrs Raxberry came running, half in, half out of her navy top.

'I'm here, Harry. It's OK, sweetie.' She took a deep breath. 'For God's sake, Keith! *I'll* sort the kids. You go and get changed.'

'Changed?'

'You're not going to wear those awful jeans to La Terrazza?'

'OK, OK.'

I couldn't understand her. Mr Raxberry looked wonderful in his jeans. Why did she treat him like an idiot all the time?

She picked Lily up. 'There now, come to Mummy. Who needs a nappy to cover her little pink bot?' she cooed in a silly voice.

Lily kicked her little legs like a frog and then weed all down Mrs Raxberry's white trousers. She squealed, and told Mr Raxberry it was all his fault. She stamped off to get changed again, a wet, squirmy Lily under one arm.

I looked at Mr Raxberry. He looked at me. We were both trying not to burst out laughing. He raised his eyebrows at me and then went off to get changed himself.

'OK, I'll read you your Gruffalo book, Harry,' I said, in a nice-bright-cheerful-nanny voice.

Harry pushed the book away peevishly and slid down the bed, half-hidden under the sheets. 'Stupid smelly big girl,' he said, entirely disappearing under the duvet.

I ducked my head under too. 'Don't mess with me, little boy,' I hissed. 'You come out and I'll tell you your story and if you're very very good I'll give you some chocolate when your mum and dad have gone out.'

'A whole big bar?' said Harry.

'Well, that depends on how good you are.'

He was positively angelic, especially when it mattered, saying goodbye to his mum and dad. I decided childcare was a piece of cake – well, bar of chocolate. If I ever had children they'd be impeccably behaved, though they'd probably be little dumplings with no teeth.

Lily was too little for bribery, but she seemed contented enough. She looked like a very tiny snowman in her small white sleeping suit. I held her on my lap as I sat on Harry's bed and made her wave her little arm to Mr and Mrs Raxberry.

'You're sure you're going to be all right, Prudence?' said Mrs Raxberry. 'You look very *young*.'

'I'm fifteen,' I said. Well, I would be next year.

144

'Oh dear, is that all?' she said doubtfully, pulling down her skirt. She was back in her skin-tight dress. 'You have done lots of babysitting before, haven't you?'

'I've been babysitting my little sister for years,' I said truthfully. 'Don't worry, we'll be fine.'

I produced the chocolate as soon as they'd gone out the front door. Harry drooled his way through the entire bar. I had to keep wiping his mouth so he wouldn't get chocolate slurp on his sheets, and when his eyelids started drooping I got his toothbrush and whisked it round his teeth as he sprawled, half asleep. He grumbled at me, but turned over on his side and rubbed his nose into the soft tummy of his teddy bear.

Lily cried a little when I carefully slid her into her wicker cot, but she calmed down when I stroked her feathery curls.

'There now,' I whispered.

I watched over the two of them for a few minutes. They'd stopped being irritating now they were asleep. They were just two sweet little children. I'd always thought I couldn't stand to have children myself but now I wasn't so sure. I imagined being Mrs Raxberry. This was my house, these were my children, he was my husband.

My heart started thumping at the thought. I tiptoed out of the children's bedroom and hovered on the landing. I peered inside the bathroom, still wet and steamy. I felt the two large, damp, navy towels, wondering which one was his. I looked at the toothbrushes in the jar and thought of his even white teeth, and the way he smiled.

I looked at the razor and imagined it gliding down his soapy cheeks, carefully stopping short of his neat beard. I looked at the hairbrush and thought of it tugging through his dark shiny hair. I looked at the two navy towelling dressing gowns hanging on the peg. They seemed identical in size. I sniffed them cautiously. One smelled faintly of face cream and hairspray.

I held the other one, his one. I fitted my arms into the sleeves and wrapped the gown round me, tying it tightly. It felt as if he was holding me, wrapping his arms round me. I closed my eyes for a moment, imagining it. When I looked in the misty mirror I almost expected him to be looking over my shoulder, smiling at me.

I took his dressing gown off reluctantly and hung it carefully back on the hook, suddenly worried that they'd been arranged in a special way.

My face was flushed, my hands were trembling. I told myself to go downstairs and start reading my book, do my homework. *I could watch television!* I knew Grace – and Mum – would want a second-by-second account of every programme I'd watched, even the adverts.

I couldn't help it. My feet were creeping along the carpet to the next door, their bedroom. I pushed the door open, holding my breath. I'm not sure what I'd imagined. It wasn't this

146

ordinary, untidy room with discarded clothes scattered over the daffodil duvet and grubby make-up spilling across the dressing table. I fingered each item curiously, opening her face cream and trying a tiny bit, dabbing her powder on my nose, daubing her pink lipstick on my lips. It tasted sickly sweet. I wondered if he liked the taste when he kissed her. *Did* he still kiss her? Of course he must do. They had children, didn't they?

I looked at their bed, half the poppers missing on their yellow duvet, the machine-embroidered flowers unravelling on their pillows, their padded headboard faded. Mr Raxberry saw everything in such sharp focus. How could he bear to sleep in this messy room?

I went to the white fitted wardrobe and opened it. Her clothes were on one side, a little rumpled, some falling off their hangers, pinks and lilacs and primrose, beige and navy and tan. His clothes were the other side, mostly black, with some blue denim. I stroked them very gently and cautiously, as if they were thoroughbred horses. I even knelt down and examined his shoes, trying them on my hands, making them do a little tap dance. He had small neat feet. I set the shoes back carefully, side by side.

I peeped inside the chest of drawers. I wanted to find special secret things but I just found underwear, socks, her tights in a brown tangle like a nest of soft snakes.

I looked at the books on either side of the bed.

Hers were pastel coloured to match her clothes, romantic tales of single women looking for true love. His books were special – a battered Penguin *David Copperfield*, a John Updike, a Hanif Kureishi. I flicked through them, wondering which were his favourite passages. I knew we had *David Copperfield* in the shop and several Updikes, and I could search for the Kureishi paperback in boot fair boxes. I could read them all and then bring them casually into one of our conversations and he'd be amazed at the similarity of our literary taste.

No, he wouldn't be fooled. He'd guess I'd sneaked into his bedroom and fingered the books by his bed. I piled them up again quickly and then backed out of the room. I checked the children again, trying to justify my presence, and then went downstairs.

I made myself a cup of coffee, taking it black and strong because it seemed more sophisticated, though it made me shudder. Then I forgot all about trying to act like an adult, becoming transfixed by the chocolates and sweets in a big earthenware bowl. Mum made toffee and fudge and truffles, but we never had a whole bowlful, not even at Christmas. I didn't imagine Mr Raxberry tucking into all the goodies. *She* was the one who had secret nibbles all day. Maybe she bribed Harry into good behaviour too.

She'd told me to help myself to anything I fancied. My fingers hovered over this and that before I selected one creamy white truffle. I rolled it round and round my mouth while I switched on the television and flicked through all the channels. I couldn't settle to watch anything. It was as if I was acting in my own highly coloured romantic drama. I needed to savour it.

I sat on the sofa, tucking my legs up, imagining what it would be like to sit there every night, the children upstairs in bed and Mr Raxberry beside me. Would we watch television, would we read our books, would we talk? Would we stay at separate ends of the sofa or would we loll against each other, cuddling up together?

I felt something hard and flat under the cushion, some little book. No, it was a sketchpad, a little Rowney one. I had the same size sketchpad at home. I opened it, holding my breath. Mr Raxberry's own private drawing book! I turned each page carefully, terrified of smudging the charcoal and chalk. There were quick sketches of the children: Harry running, riding his toddler bike, watching television with his teddy under his chin. There were sketches of Lily too, lying on her back kicking, propped in her highchair nibbling toast, laughing uproariously, her eyes squeezed shut and her mouth wide open.

There were several sketches of Mrs Raxberry feeding Lily, telling Harry a story, and one of her on her own. She was lying stretched out on the sofa, one arm above her head, the pose smoothing out her thick waist and large stomach so that she just looked lush and womanly.

I frowned at the picture. It was so tender and intimate, even though she was fully dressed. I wanted to rip it out of the book. I forced myself to flip past it. There were plant studies, bowls of fruit, a tree, and several sketches of the school, as seen from the art-room window. There were sketches of some of the pupils – a lovely one of Sarah laughing as she daubed thick paint.

Then I turned the page and saw a portrait of a thin girl with thick curly hair, a girl with big dark eyes gazing intently into space, in her own imaginary world. The girl was wearing a dress, the check pattern lightly suggested.

It was me.

They came home just after eleven.

'How were the kids? Did they wake? Did you give Lily her bottle? Did Harry want you to read to him?' Mrs Raxberry said in a rush as she burst through the door.

'They've been fine,' I said. 'Lily cried around ten and I warmed her bottle, but she was asleep again before I could feed her. There hasn't been a peep out of Harry.'

'Great, great! I'd better go and wake him for a wee then, otherwise we'll have a wet bed. Here's your money, Prue. Thanks so much. I hope you can maybe babysit again some time?'

I took a deep breath. 'I'd love to.' I shrugged on my jacket and went into the hall. I didn't even make eye contact with Mr Raxberry. I felt as if I'd been snuggled up with him all evening.

If I so much as glanced at the real man I was sure I would blush.

'Hey, where are you going, Prue?' he called after me.

'Home.'

'Well, hang on, I'm giving you a lift.'

It was what I'd been thinking about ever since I agreed to babysit, but now I felt weirdly scared.

'No, no, it's OK. I'll get the bus. It's not far, I'll be fine, honestly. Bye!' I burbled.

'I'm taking you home in the car,' Mr Raxberry said firmly. 'Stop arguing.'

So I stopped. I called goodbye to his wife and then Mr Raxberry and I walked down his garden path together.

'Here we are,' he said, opening the car door for me. 'Oh God, excuse the kids' rubbish. We don't even notice it any more.'

I kicked several juice cartons, a little truck and a set of plastic keys out of my way and sat in the front seat. Mr Raxberry got in the driver's seat.

'Seat belt,' he said to me.

I stared at him, I looked at my lap, I dithered anxiously. I'd been driven in a car so rarely I didn't know how to use a seat belt. Dad had once run a van for book-buying expeditions, but had rarely taken us out as a family. When the van needed a new gearbox several years ago he'd had to scrap it.

Mr Raxberry leaned towards me. For one mad magical moment I thought he was going to kiss me. Then he reached past me and pulled on a strap. He was simply fixing my seat belt for me.

'There now, safely strapped in,' he said, starting up the car. 'What did you do with yourself this evening, then?'

I blushed, but it was mercifully dark in the car. 'Oh, I read a bit, did a little homework. Whatever,' I said vaguely.

'I hope it wasn't too lonely for you. You can always bring a friend with you another time, or maybe your sister?' he said lightly.

'No! No, I'm fine by myself, I don't mind a bit,' I said quickly.

He looked over at me, nodding. 'I know. I liked my own company as a kid too. I used to go fishing most weekends. It wasn't to catch the fish; I used to feel sick and sorry if I ever *caught* anything. I just wanted to be by myself for a bit.'

'Do you still go fishing now?'

'Chance would be a fine thing! At the weekends we do the Sainsbury's run, and then I look after the kids while Marianne sees her girlfriends, and then on Sunday we drive all the way to Basingstoke to see her parents for a Sunday roast, and often Marianne's sister's there with *her* husband and kids, so we're all very busy playing Happy Families.' He kept his voice very light and even. I didn't know whether he was happy or bitter or bored, and I couldn't really ask.

We only had about ten minutes together and

there was so much I wanted to ask him. But everything I wanted to know was too direct, too personal.

Do you think I'm really any good at art?

Do you like me?

Why did you draw me in your secret sketchbook?

Instead, I chattered childishly about fishing, asking about lines and hooks and bait, as if I *cared*. I felt as helpless as a fish on the end of a line myself. He was reeling me in tighter and tighter until I was out of my element.

We turned into my street and I gave him directions to the shop.

'Oh, it's *this* shop! I've been here. I've had a good browse in the art section, but someone gave me a sarcastic ticking off for using the shop like a library.' He paused. 'Would that have been your dad?'

'That would *definitely* have been my dad,' I said. 'No wonder we have hardly any customers. He's always so rude to them.'

'How *is* your dad?'

'Well, he can't talk much still, and he can't really walk either.' I sniffed, suddenly near tears, feeling guilty because he'd have given Mum and Grace such a hard time at the hospital tonight.

Mr Raxberry didn't quite understand. 'Oh Prue, I'm so sorry,' he said. His hand reached out and covered mine.

The car took off like a rocket, soaring into space,

154

whirling up and over the moon, his hand on mine, his hand on mine, his hand on mine . . .

He gave my hand a gentle squeeze, and then put his own hand back on the steering wheel. The car hurtled back into the earthly atmosphere. He drummed his fingers on the wheel. We sat still, neither of us saying anything, staring straight ahead.

'Well,' he said. I heard him swallow. 'Perhaps you'd better go in now.'

'Yes. Thank you for taking me home, Mr Raxberry.'

That made him look at me. 'Hey, what's with this formal Mr Raxberry thing? Everyone at school calls me Rax – you know that.'

'OK then. Rax.' I giggled. 'It sounds funny.'

'Better than Keith.'

'Why doesn't your wife call you Rax?'

'Oh. She's known me too long. We were childhood sweethearts.'

I wasn't sure whether this was a good thing or not. 'You knew each other when you were at school?'

'From when we were fourteen.'

'*My* age?'

'Yep.'

'Goodness.'

'I take it you haven't got a sweetheart?'

'No!'

'I'm glad to hear it. Off you go then. See you at school.'

'Yes. Thank you. Goodbye . . . Rax.' I giggled

again and then undid my seat belt and jumped out of the car. He waited until I let myself in the shop door. I turned and waved and he waved back and then drove off.

I wanted to stay in the dark shop, breathing in the musty smell of old books, going over our car ride again and again, remembering every word, every gesture, every touch. I could hear Mum calling me from her bedroom, fearful at first in case I might be a burglar, though what self-respecting thief would want crumpled Catherine Cookson paperbacks, battered Ladybirds, leatherette Reader's Digest compilations and £4.99 in the till?

'Prudence? Is that you?'

No, Mum, I'm not me any more. I'm this new girl flying above the dusty floor. I want to stay up up up in the air.

I heard the creak of her bed, then the stomp stomp of her slippered feet. There was a patter from Grace too, and the bang of our bedroom door as she flung it open. I sighed and started up the stairs.

I told them all about the house and the furniture and the children and the wife and the television programmes. Then I pressed the five-pound notes into Mum's hand.

'But it's *your* money, Prue!'

'I want to pay you back for the maths tuition money.'

'You're such a good girl,' she said, making me feel *bad*.

I kissed her goodnight and went to bed. Grace started asking me all sorts of questions, but I told her I was too tired to start answering anything. I lay flat on my back, staring at the ceiling in the dark. I wondered if he was lying likewise, or whether he slept curled round his wife.

'Prue! *Please* tell me how you got on with Rax,' Grace whispered.

I pretended to be asleep.

'*Prue!*'

I still didn't answer. She got out of her own bed and tried to clamber into mine.

'Prue, tell me, what did he say on the way home?' she whispered, her hair in my face, her big soft body pressed against mine.

'You're squashing me! Move *over*. I was asleep.'

'No you weren't. You can't fool me, Prue. You're nuts about him, aren't you?'

'Of course I'm not. He's a boring old *teacher*, years and years older than me, and he's married with two children.'

'Yes, but you still fancy him.'

'No, I *don't*,' I said, and I pushed her out of bed.

'You do,' she said, sprawled on the floor. 'Ouch! I think you're nuts. You could have any boy you want. You could even have Toby Baker, yet you want old Rax!'

I pulled the covers over my head. I couldn't hear her any more. I just heard my own thoughts, drumming in my head like the blood at my temple.

I hardly slept but I got up early and cleaned and swept the shop. I carefully dusted Dad's Magnum Opus, and then spent ages copying out the first few sentences in large print, wondering if Dad might be able to read it and then say the words out loud – words he'd been composing half his life, chanting them under his breath as if they were a holy mantra.

'That's your dad's book! Careful with it. What are you doing?' Mum fussed.

I sighed and explained.

'Oh Prue! What a good idea! Why didn't I think of that. You're *so* clever.'

'Tell that to my teachers,' I said. 'They all think I'm thick thick thick.'

'Well, this Mr Raxberry can't think that or he'd never leave you in charge of his kiddies,' said Mum.

I ducked my head so she couldn't see I was blushing. I worked on Dad's book while Mum stood downstairs in the empty shop and Grace spent hours on the phone chatting to Iggy and Figgy. I flipped through Dad's various notebooks and stray pieces of paper and scrapbooks and journals, trying to pick out key passages. I stared at his small, cramped, backward-sloping scribble until my eyes blurred.

I still didn't really *understand* it. I'd thought it way above my head. Now I read it carefully, page after page, and I realized something so sad. It wasn't really difficult at all. There was no extraordinary philosophical theory, no dynamic take on the human condition, no overriding theme, no new angle. It was just Dad rambling and ranting. It held no meaning for anyone but himself. Maybe it didn't even hold any meaning for him now.

I closed his book, wanting to hide it away. It exposed Dad too painfully. It was like looking at him in his baggy underwear.

'Prue? Can you come down a minute?' Mum was shouting at me from the shop.

I didn't take any notice.

'*Prue!* Will you come down here? There's someone asking for you!'

I leaped up and went flying down the stairs, combing my hair with my fingers, tugging at my awful dress, wishing I had some decent clothes, wanting to check myself in the mirror but terrified he'd give up and go if I kept him waiting any longer.

I stumbled into the shop, cheeks burning, scarcely able to breathe. I looked all round. He wasn't there. I blinked. Mum came into focus, gesturing at some stupid boy standing by the door. Not some boy, any old boy. It was Toby Baker.

I sighed. 'Oh, it's you,' I said ungraciously.

'Hi, Prue,' he said, not at all put out. 'How are you doing?'

I stared at him as if he was mad.

'Your mum says she doesn't need you to work in the shop this morning, so I thought we could maybe do that tuition thing. You know, me help you with your maths and you could hear me do a bit of reading. I've got my books with me.' He patted his rucksack.

'Isn't that lovely!' said Mum. 'Well, where would you two like to work? I suppose you could always sit at your dad's desk, Prue.'

'No, I thought we could go out somewhere in the town, McDonald's maybe, and have a cup of coffee first. We'd kind of relax then, so it wouldn't be like a school situation,' Toby said.

Mum nodded, mesmerized by his blond good looks and sweet manners. I heard a little gasp behind me. Grace had come running downstairs after me and was gawping at him. Her fingers twitched to start dialling Iggy and Figgy on the phone.

'Sorry, Toby, I can't,' I said. 'I've got stuff to do.'

'No you *haven't*,' Grace said.

'You've been a lovely helpful girl. You can go and relax a bit now,' said Mum. She looked worried, but she added determinedly, 'I think it's an excellent idea you two getting together and helping each other with your lessons.'

I didn't want to at all, but I couldn't say so right to Toby's face. I mumbled my way through several more excuses, none of which held up – and ended up being dispatched towards the town with Toby.

'I can't stay long though,' I said.

I'd got it into my head that Rax *might* just come by the shop, maybe while his wife was trailing round Sainsbury's. I'd die if I missed him.

I rather hoped all this tuition nonsense was a ploy and that Toby would try to drag me somewhere quiet to kiss me. Then I could simply shove him off me and run back to the shop. But to my irritation he seemed determined to behave perfectly, keeping a little distance between us as we walked into town, talking earnestly about his dyslexia and how he'd felt so humiliated as a little kid and he'd hated books so much he'd scribbled all over his sister's paperbacks.

I made all the right responses but it was such an effort I started to get a headache. However, there was a little bit of me that was pleased a boy like Toby seemed to like me. As we got nearer the town centre little gangs of girls going shopping looked round and stared enviously. They raised their eyebrows at my Saturday outfit. I was wearing last year's dreadful blue cord dress, which was way too short for me, and a shapeless hand-knitted purple sweater that had stretched in the wash. I'd threaded blue and purple glass beads into a strand of my hair and painted a blue cornflower on one of my old black shoes and a purple daisy on the other. I was worried that these homespun embellishments made me look weirder than ever.

Toby had made a serious effort. His shirt was always hanging out at school, his tie undone, his shoes unlaced, but now he was wearing a hooded jacket with a coveted logo, black sweater and black jeans so obviously new he could barely bend his legs. He'd just washed his famously floppy blond hair. It fell silkily over his forehead into his eyes, so he had to keep shaking his head every so often. I knew all the girls at Wentworth thought this a fabulously sexy gesture, but I was starting to find it intensely irritating.

We went to the McDonald's in the shopping centre. Toby insisted on buying us two Cokes, plus two portions of french fries. I thought of Grace and how she'd die for a chance to sample McDonald's chips.

Toby manoeuvred us to a table right at the back and then opened his rucksack. He really did have half a dozen textbooks and two pads of paper tucked inside.

'OK, I thought I could maybe talk you through some basic maths. Not that I'm any great shakes, mind, but I'll help if I can.'

'Please don't,' I said. 'I mean, it's very nice of you, but I *hate* maths. I don't want to do it.'

'But you'll have to master it sometime.'

'No I won't. I can do enough. How many people are sitting at this table? Two. How many Cokes have they got? Two. How many chips have they got left?' I helped myself to a handful. 'Not many at this rate.'

'You're so different from all the other girls, Prue. I really reckon you, you know that.'

'Don't start all that. Look, I'll help you with your reading if that's what you really want. Get your book out.'

He brought out this grim little reader in big

print with cartoon pictures of teenagers and a lot of stilted phrases and dated slang.

'Oh God,' I said.

'It's not *my* fault. It's better than some of the others – Peter and Jane and Pat the flipping dog.'

'OK then, get cracking. *The Big Match*. Start!'

'I feel a fool. OK, OK. *The – Big – Match*. Why does match have a "t" in it anyway? It's stupid. Right. *The – Big – Match*.'

'You've *said* that. And I've said it too. Now start on the rest.'

He started. I realized how bad he really was at reading. I thought he'd just trip up on a few of the longer words, maybe mix up the odd *were* or *where*, the way Grace used to when she was five or six. But Toby was still way back at the beginning stage, stumbling through each and every word. It was as if the letters grew into tall trees and he was blundering through a dense forest, unable to find his way out.

I sat and listened. I helped him out, prompting him, sometimes taking over and reading out a whole phrase. I kept my voice gentle, neutral, encouraging, the voice I used for coaching Dad. Toby was much sweeter natured. He kept apologizing, thanking me over and over, telling me I was a born teacher. He thought I was being so kind because I really cared, when inside my head I was hot, angry, bored. I listened to him stuttering away and I had to press my lips together to stop myself screaming at him.

When he eventually made it all the way through the story and Bil-ly had fi-nal-ly got tick-ets for the Big Match we both cheered as if Toby had scored a goal.

'Wow! That's the first book I've ever read all the way through!' he said.

He was flushed with pride at his achievement, even though *The Big Match* wasn't really a *book* and I'd told him three-quarters of the words.

'It's all down to you,' he said, and he squeezed my hand.

I snatched it away quickly. I didn't want anyone else holding my hand now. I stuck it into the empty french fries packet, pretending to be looking for a last chip.

'We'll some more! And a burger? Or are you more an ice-cream kind of girl?'

'No, no, I don't want anything, really,' I said. 'I've got to get going. Mum will need me to help in the shop.'

'She said it was fine. I'm sure you can stay out longer. We really ought to give you a bit of maths tuition now.'

'I *said*. No!'

'Well then, we could go round the shopping centre if you want. Anywhere you like, I don't mind. Even clothes shops.'

'There's not much point my going round any clothes shops. I haven't got any money for any decent clothes.'

'I thought girls just liked to look. Rita always wants to spend *hours* in New Look and TopShop.'

I fingered my awful sweater defensively. 'I know I look a freak,' I mumbled.

'You don't. I love the way you look. You're not boring like all the other girls, you've got your *own* style.'

'Yeah, part jumble sale, part botched home-made,' I said.

I was pleased all the same. I hoped Rax felt like that about me too. I wondered if he ever took his wife and kids to McDonald's on their Saturday morning shopping trips. I wanted to see him so much. If he spotted me with Toby he'd realize I wasn't completely a sad little Prudence-No-Friends.

I supposed I counted Toby as a friend now, just so long as he didn't try to be anything more.

I wandered round the shopping centre with him for half an hour, but I couldn't really say I enjoyed myself. Toby was very eager to please, shuffling along one pace behind me so I had to keep choosing where we were going. I didn't know which shops to amble in and out of, how long to take admiring different outfits, which racks to spin with interest. It all seemed so false and uncomfortable and awkward. I tried hard to keep up a steady stream of chatter. His answers were mostly monosyllabic. Maybe he was used to small simple words, like the ones in his reading book.

I seemed to be fated to help people with their reading. It had been tedious with Toby but it was far worse with Dad. He was clearly furious with me for not turning up on Friday. He wanted to interrogate me but couldn't find the words. He came out with a long semi-comprehensible splutter: 'Baby? – No! – *Not!*' I knew he was expressly forbidding me to do such a thing again but I chose to misunderstand.

'Yes, Dad, I simply wanted to start earning some money of my own. I'm so glad you think it's a good idea,' I said.

Dad reached boiling point, straining to say what he meant. He thumped the bed with his left arm. He even did a feeble mini thump with his right.

'Oh Arthur, you're really getting lots of

movement back now!' Mum said, clutching his bad hand and stroking it.

Dad snatched it away from her, not wanting to be distracted. 'Baby – no-no-no!' he repeated.

'Yes, Dad. Lily's the baby, and Harry's the little boy. They can be a bit of a handful, but I can get them sorted out. Just call me Mary Poppins, eh?'

Dad looked as if he wanted to call me all sorts of names, though Mary Poppins wasn't one of them. But then I took out the compilation I'd made of extracts from his Magnum Opus. The moment I read out the first line Dad lay still. He listened, his head cocked to one side, his mouth snapped back into a straight line. He looked almost his old self.

'Now you try to read a little, Dad,' I said.

He reached for the book. He cleared his throat. He pronounced the first four words clearly, with proper expression. I thought a miracle had happened. Dad had recovered all his faculties and I could stop feeling chewed up with guilt. But then he stumbled, he repeated himself, he couldn't get any further though he strained to the utmost. His entire Magnum Opus was reduced to four words: *I, Bernard King, think . . .*

Dad's eyes filled with tears.

'Oh Prue, don't upset him! Maybe you should put it away,' Mum whispered.

'Don't worry, Dad. I'm sure you'll be able to read it all soon. Meanwhile, I'll read it, shall I?'

Dad nodded, and so I read to him. He twitched

and sniffled for a minute or two and then he became absorbed. Grace yawned and twiddled her thumbs and did mini Iggy-Figgy waves to herself. Mum frowned at her as if she was fidgeting in church. She had an expression of pious concentration on her face but her eyes were darting all round the room. I knew she was thinking about Dad's washing and cooking our tea and all the final demands and bailiff's threats at home.

I read on, my voice starting to mimic Dad's old intonations and accent as I worked my way through his convoluted sentences. I started to ham it up just a little, inserting a Dad-cough here and a Dad-sniff there. Mum glared. Grace snorted. Dad snorted too, regularly, again and again. He was fast asleep and snoring. His Magnum Opus had worked like a bedtime story for a tired toddler.

I left my cut-price annotated version on his bedside locker. I hoped Dad might enjoy glancing at it, but when we visited on Sunday it was missing. I asked him about it but Dad looked blank and shook his head. So much for my labour of love. One of the cleaners had obviously chucked it in the rubbish bin. Dad had forgotten all about it.

I'd been going to copy out more of it, maybe even do a couple of watercolour illustrations, but now I decided not to bother.

I hid myself away on Sunday evening, constructing a surreal sculpture based on our old doll's house. I made a papier-mâché man, deliberately too big for the house. His arms reached out of the windows, his feet stuck out of the door, his head was halfway out of the chimney, but he couldn't escape, try as he might. I fashioned a fat fur mouse out of an old pair of mittens, and made two tiny mice from each thumb. The man had a collar round his neck. The fat mouse had the lead tightly clasped in her paws. The two tiny mice scrabbled on his shoulders, shrieking in his ears.

Grace crept up on me and peered over my shoulder. 'That's good – but *weird*,' she said. 'It's like that Alice book. *Is* it Alice?'

Dad had once discovered what he thought was a first edition of *Alice in Wonderland* at a jumble sale and thought it would make our fortune, but of course it wasn't a *real* first edition, just an illustrated edition from much later that was hardly worth a bean. Dad couldn't bear to see it on the shelf in the shop and gave it to me as a colouring book.

'Yes, it's Alice,' I said to Grace.

How could she be idiotic enough to think I'd give Alice a *beard*?

'Is it for homework?'

'Sort of.'

'Have you done all your other homework?'

'Nope.'

'Hadn't you better get cracking?'

'I'm not doing it.'

'You'll get into trouble.'

'See if I care.'

I *did* get into trouble on Monday, but it wasn't over homework. I got to school early, wandered across the playground, walked over to the playing field and hovered near the art block. I hoped that Rax might be at school early too, but his art room was in darkness and there was no sign of him. I sighed and started trailing back towards the main building. We didn't have art on Monday. I had a dreaded maths session in the Success Maker.

I looked longingly at the school gate, wondering whether to make a run for it. Rita was flouncing through the gate into school, tossing her head, obviously sounding off about something to her friends, Aimee, Megan and Jess. Then she looked up and saw someone. She started running forwards, her pretty face contorted. I looked round. There was no one behind me. She was angry with *me*.

'You cow! You scheming lying cheating little *cow*!' she screamed right in my face.

I stepped back, because she was spraying me with spit.

'Don't you *dare* back away from me!' she yelled. She seized a handful of my hair and tugged hard.

'Stop it! Get off!' I said. 'Have you gone mad?'

'You're the mad girl, thinking you can mess around with me by stealing my boyfriend!'

'I *haven't* stolen your stupid boyfriend,' I said, jerking my head to make her let go.

'You liar! I saw you with him in McDonald's,' said Aimee. 'You were right at the back, cuddling up to him, practically sitting on his lap, hanging on his every word.'

'I was listening to him *read*,' I said.

'Oh yeah, and I can read *you* like a book,' cried Rita. 'You set out to get him away from me the moment you came barging into our school in your stupid sad dresses and your slag's underwear. How *dare* you! Me and Toby have had a thing going ever since Year Eight. He's *mine*, everyone knows that.'

'OK, OK. He's yours. *I* don't want him,' I said. 'I don't even like him.'

'*What?* Toby's the only decent boy in our year. Everyone reckons him!'

'Well, not me. So I don't know why you're making such a stupid fuss. You can keep him.'

'You *know* he's broken up with me!' Rita said, and she started crying.

Aimee and Megan and Jess had all been egging her on, enjoying the fight, but now they clucked round her like mother hens.

'He told me it's all over. He says he still wants to be my friend but he doesn't love me any more. He tried to smooth his way out of things but I soon got the whole story out of him. It's all because of *you*, Prudence King!'

They all looked at me accusingly.

'I haven't done anything!' I said.

'He says you talk together, that you say all sorts of stuff. What have you been telling him?'

'Nothing! Well, nothing special. Look, Rita, I swear I didn't know he was going to break up with you. It's not *my* fault.' I tried to say it calmly and reasonably but my heart was thumping hard. Maybe it *was* my fault, just a little bit? It was awful seeing Rita crying like that, tears dribbling down her face, her nose running, with everyone staring at her.

I held out my hand. 'I'm sorry,' I said.

She stared at me, her face all screwed up, almost ugly. 'Don't you *dare* feel sorry for me!' she said, and she flew at me and slapped my face.

I slapped her back, just as hard.

'Fight, fight, fight!' the girls yelled.

Rita and I hit out at each other, slapping, scratching, tugging hair, tearing at each other's clothes, toppling over and rolling on the floor.

'Prudence King, Rita Rogers, stop scrapping this *instant*!'

It was Miss Wilmott. She grabbed Rita by one wrist, me by the other, and pulled us both up. 'Whatever's got into you! Fighting like gutter children and yet you're both in Year Ten! What sort of behaviour *is* this?'

'Prue stole Rita's boyfriend, miss,' said Aimee. 'It's all Prue's fault.'

'I don't care whose fault it is. I'm not having any pupils of Wentworth behaving like animals, especially not over boyfriends!' said Miss Wilmott. 'Go and tidy yourselves up, girls, and then come and stand outside my office. You're both in very serious trouble.'

We ended up having to spend the entire morning outside her office, me standing on one side of the door, Rita the other, in public disgrace. We weren't supposed to look at each other, but whenever I glanced Rita's way she seemed to be in tears.

I didn't particularly mind standing there. It was certainly preferable to maths. I'd have liked to be able to read, but that couldn't be helped. I held long conversations in my head with Jane instead. I didn't want to talk to Tobias. I wanted to steer clear of all boys, even imaginary ones.

Every now and then the bell went and pupils charged past us, rushing up and down the corridor. They stared at Rita, they stared at me. Rita's friends had obviously been talking. It was clear from the black looks directed at me whose side everyone was on.

Form 10 EL ambled past on their way to a music lesson in the hall. There was a lot of nudging, a lot of shoving. The girls hissed 'Slag slag slag' at me, like an incantation. The boys whooped and laughed and strutted, thrilled that two girls had been fighting over one of them. The only boy who shuffled past, head down, was Toby.

He looked at me anxiously and mouthed 'I'm sorry'.

I put my head down and stared at the scuffed wooden floor, not wanting to respond. He hovered in front of me a moment or two, but then moved on. I kept my eyes on the floor as if I was learning the pattern of the parquet by heart. He paused in front of Rita too. Her sniffles increased.

I stared down resolutely. There were further footsteps. They stopped in front of me. I saw black canvas boots, black jeans. I looked up. There was Rax, his head tilted, one eyebrow raised.

'Are you in disgrace?' he said.

I nodded. He made little tutting noises, showing he wasn't taking it at all seriously. I longed to talk to him but I didn't want Rita to listen. Rax understood. He gave me a sympathetic smile and then walked on. He tutted at Rita in a friendly fashion too, but not in the same way.

I looked up to watch him walk the length of the corridor. He turned round at the end and gave me a quick wave.

I couldn't wait to talk to him properly in the art class on Tuesday. I worked hard on my still life, adding shadows and highlights. Rita kept out of my way, but Aimee and Megan and Jess kept barging past, trying to jog me. I learned not to paint when they were anywhere near me.

Even Daisy turned on me. She came and peered over my shoulder. 'You think you're so great, Prudence Slag, but that painting's rubbish.'

Sarah didn't say anything nasty but she didn't smile at me any more. They'd all decided to hate me. Even Toby kept his distance, right at the other end of the classroom, but I'd made it clear enough I didn't want to talk to him.

Rax didn't seem to notice. He didn't really seem

174

to notice *me*, just giving me the occasional nod or brief tip: 'Try a glimmer of white there . . .'; 'Is that shadow really black? What other colours is it made of?'; 'Maybe you want to suggest the book titles, rather than actually print them out?'

I listened, I nodded, I did what he said, but inside I was dying. Why wasn't he talking *properly*? He spent ages chatting to all the others. He didn't just say arty stuff, he talked football with the boys and rock bands with the girls. He stood beside Rita and Aimee and talked for a full ten minutes. I couldn't hear what he was saying. It must have been amazing because they kept giggling. Rita stopped looking mean and miserable and laughed and joked with him, batting her long black eyelashes.

Maybe Rax had decided he was on Rita's side. Perhaps he thought I'd deliberately lured Toby away from her. Maybe he hated me now like everyone else.

I hunched over my still life, blinking hard, finding it difficult to focus. I concentrated on not crying for the rest of the lesson. As soon as the bell went I flung my brush down, not even bothering to clean it, grabbed my bag and bolted for the door.

I was right out in the playground when I heard him shouting my name.

'Prue! Prue King, come back!'

I wondered about making a bolt for it, but I trudged slowly back.

'You don't just throw your brushes down all

clogged up with paint!' said Rax. 'Come on, you know better than that. You can help me clear up all the paint pots too.'

'Serves you right, slag,' said Rita, and Aimee and Megan and Jess all made faces at me.

I started washing out brushes at the sink, my back to everyone. I couldn't stop a tear dribbling down my cheek.

'Hey, you're not crying, are you?' Rax said. 'Oh Prue, you didn't think I was cross with you, did you?'

I nodded, the tears spurting now.

'Don't!' He picked up a cloth and gently dabbed at my eyes. 'Whoops! Now you've got black paint on your eyes. You'll look like Lovely Rita if you don't watch out.'

'*Lovely* Rita?'

'Like the Beatles song.' He sang a line or two about a meter maid. 'So, what on earth's been going on between you two? Why is everyone treating you as if you've got bubonic plague?'

'They think I stole Toby away from Rita.'

'And did you?'

'*No!* Well, not really. I did go to McDonald's with him, but just to help him with his reading. It was all his idea.'

'I bet it was. So you're in the doghouse with everyone now?'

'They didn't like me much before but now they positively hate me. And I thought you did too, because you hardly talked to me at all and yet you spent ages with Rita.'

176

'Yes, because if I'd made a big fuss of you and your wonderful painting it wouldn't really have increased your popularity. What would you like me to do, Prue? Shall I have a word with Miss Wilmott?'

'No!'

'What about your form teacher?'

'Absolutely not.'

'There's meant to be a student counselling service now, one of Miss Wilmott's new ideas for Wentworth. You could have a chat with them.'

'I don't want to have a chat with *anyone*, thank you,' I said, swilling out the sink. 'I'm fine. I don't care about them.'

'You were crying.'

'I was crying because I thought *you* were cross with me.'

'I'm not cross with you.' There was a little pause. 'Anything but.'

Then he started putting the paint jars away with unnecessary fuss and clatter, not looking at me.

'So, are you able to babysit again this Friday?' he said.

'Yes please.'

'Then it's a date.'

Fridays started to feel like *real* dates. I'd rush home from school to put the immersion on for a bath. Mum always moaned about the waste of hot water, but I took no notice. I wished I had proper bath oil, scented soap, special shampoo.

Mum bought bumper packs of the cheapest brands of soap, and until I protested bitterly she expected us to do our hair with washing-up liquid.

I longed for decent clothes to wear once I was scrubbed and shampooed. I'd saved up enough babysitting money for a green skirt and sweater, and Mum had found a boy's white shirt at a jumble sale so I was in an approximation of school uniform now. (Grace got lucky too. Figgy had a large lumpy cousin in Year Eleven and she passed her entire old uniform on to Grace.)

I generally wore my school skirt to Rax's, with a black jumble jumper, weird black and green striped tights (seconds) from the one pound shop, and my customized painted black shoes. I tried different hairstyles: beaded plaits; odd bunches tied with black velvet ribbon; scraped back with little butterfly slides. I didn't have proper make-up but I experimented with my watercolours, shadowing my eyes with purple. Once I painted tiny blue stars on my earlobes; another time a daisy bracelet in china-white and emerald all round my left wrist.

'For heaven's sake, it looks as if you've got a tattoo!' Mum fussed. 'Whatever will your teacher *think*!'

He seemed to like the way I looked. He always noticed and admired each new improvisation, although one evening he said he still had a soft spot for the red-checked tablecloth dress.

I wore it the next time, with the red cardigan,

a red rose plastic slide, and my lips painted carmine. I tried painting my cheeks too but I looked like a Dutch doll so I scrubbed them clean again. I didn't need anything to act as rouge. I blushed enough naturally whenever I was with Rax.

The children had got used to me now. I didn't have to bribe Harry any more. I played Gruffalo games with him, making up my own extra adventures, sometimes drawing his favourite bits for him. Lily was too little for stories, but she liked a special Peepo game, chuckling again and again whenever I bobbed out behind a cushion.

'You've really got a way with the kids,' said Marianne. 'They like you so much, Prue.'

Marianne seemed to like me too. She'd chat to me as she was getting ready, discussing diets and hairstyles and clothes. I switched off while she rattled on, but whenever she mentioned Rax she had my full attention. She always seemed to put him down, sighing about him as if he was an exceptionally stupid child.

'It would make much more sense if he took over the childcare while I went back to my accountancy work, but he's so hopeless he'd never cope. The kids play him up anyway, especially Harry. I don't know how he manages at school.'

'He's a brilliant teacher. Everyone loves him,' I said.

'Oh, come on, Prue, I bet everyone takes the mickey. He's so *stupid* wasting his time teaching, and it's crap money anyway. He earned double that amount when he worked at the advertising agency – no, *triple*. But of course he didn't find that *creative* enough, though it beats me what's creative about giving out pots of paint to a lot of bored teenagers. Sorry, I don't mean *you*, Prue, I know you're very talented – Keith keeps telling me.'

'Does he?' I said eagerly.

'You must know he thinks the world of you,' said Marianne.

I hoped he did, but I wanted her to keep on telling me. It made me feel strange though, horribly guilty. She seemed to have no idea how I felt about Rax. She started treating me as if I was her *friend*.

'It's so good of you to babysit on a regular basis like this, Prue. Keith and I had got out of the habit of going out together. We don't really *do* much, but it does us both good. It gives me a chance to dress up a bit and feel like a human being again – and it's cheered Keith up too. I know he keeps up a smiley front at school, but he's been really down the last few months. Well, since before Lily was born. He's never said as much, even to me, but he gets these moods. But now he's much cheerier, more like the *old* Keith.' She sighed. 'Make the most of being young and having your freedom, Prue.'

I nodded politely, though I didn't want to be young, I didn't want to be free.

Rax scarcely said anything to me in front of Marianne and the children. He waited until we were alone, in the car driving home. We had ten minutes together, twenty if we stayed chatting in the car outside the shop.

We talked about art, we talked about books. Rax kept scribbling down recommendations and I kept all his notes tucked inside my copy of *Jane Eyre*, treasuring old Sainsbury's receipts and Cadbury's wrappers because they bore a few words of his beautiful italic writing. But the best conversations were when he stopped acting like my teacher and I got him to talk about himself. He shied away from talking about the way he felt *now*, but he talked easily enough about his childhood.

He told me about his first big box of felt-tip pens and how he'd spent hours kneeling up at the kitchen table, colouring the seaside with big white-tipped waves and little red boats and v-shaped seagulls flying round and round the rays of his yellow sun. He drew himself standing on a rock licking a giant strawberry ice cream with chocolate flakes sticking out like horns. His mother had entered it for a children's art competition and it had come second.

'Another boy at my school came first, and I couldn't help minding dreadfully. I managed not to show it in front of him, but I cried at home – how pathetic is that!'

'But very understandable.'

'My mum understood too, and had my picture specially framed. I think she's still got it hanging in her kitchen.'

181

'Has she got any of your later work, things you did at art school or afterwards?'

'No, I think she feels I went off dreadfully after the age of seven. She may well be right.'

'And do you still like strawberry ice cream with chocolate flakes?'

'You bet I do!'

Then we got onto our favourite foods. Rax couldn't believe I'd never eaten a pizza or a chop suey or a chicken tandoori.

'I'll have to treat you sometime,' he said.

'Yes please!'

I kept hoping that he'd suggest a *specific* time, but he was probably just playing a game. Sometimes he treated me like a little kid, as if I wasn't much older than Harry. I tried to behave in a sophisticated manner, but sometimes he teased me when I used an elaborate phrase or struck a pose.

'Don't laugh at me,' I said, stung.

'I'm not laughing. Well. Just a little bit,' he said.

'I'm simply trying to impress you,' I said.

'You don't have to try, Prue. You do that already,' he said.

'Really?'

'You're a funny kid.'

'I'm not funny. And I'm *not* a kid,' I said, flouncing out of the car.

'Hey! Don't go off in a huff!' he said, winding down his window.

I stuck my head back inside. 'Who's huffy? Not me!' I said. Then I blew him a little kiss goodbye.

I didn't touch him. It was just a silly little gesture. He didn't need to take it seriously — though I wanted him to.

He wasn't quite so chatty this last time, driving me home. I tried hard to introduce interesting topics of conversation, but nothing really seemed to spark with him. We got home much too soon.

'Perhaps you could park the car up the road a bit instead of just outside the shop?' I suggested. 'If Mum hears the car she'll wonder why I'm not coming in straight away.'

'And why *aren't* you coming in straight away?' said Rax.

'Because I want to talk to you!'

'I know, I know. And I want to talk to you too, Prue. But . . . but we're starting to act as if . . . as if there's something between us.'

'There is,' I said.

'Well, yes, I know we get on really well, and it's a privilege for me to help you with your art, but that's all it can be, Prue. You do know that, don't you?'

'I know. But what do you *really* want inside? What if you weren't my teacher?'

'It doesn't matter what I feel inside.'

'It matters to me. *You* matter to me.'

'Don't, Prue. Look, this is all my fault. I should have kept my distance. You're going through a difficult time, you're feeling very vulnerable, your dad's not well. It's not surprising you've got overly attached to me.'

'I'm not *attached*.' I took a deep breath. 'I love you, you know I do.'

'Prue. Look, you're a very sweet girl—'

'Don't treat me like Sarah.'

'Oh dear God.' He put his head in his hands, resting against the steering wheel.

'It's all right,' I said. 'I won't make things difficult for you. I won't tell anyone else the way I feel. I won't do anything at all. But please, won't you tell me if you love me just a little bit?'

'I'm married, I've got two small children. I'm a teacher, you're my pupil – you're fourteen years old, for God's sake.'

'Do you love me?'

'Prue, please, stop this. Go indoors now, your mother will be wondering where you are. Off you go.'

He waited until I was safely out of the car, standing on the pavement. Then he whispered one word as he drove away. I couldn't hear him, of course, but I saw his face clearly in the lamplight. He said yes.

Yes yes yes yes yes yes yes yes yes yes yes yes.

14

Rax seemed to be avoiding me at school. He barely nodded when we passed in the corridor. When I started a new project in art he didn't even comment. We'd started working on aspects of Christmas. I found his postcard of a Botticelli Nativity and I made a fair stab at copying it, using gouache for the first time. I did a little replica Mary, Jesus and Joseph, I painted all their visitors, rural and exotic, and the holy livestock, and used up a lot of pink and gold on the host of heavenly angels circling the cattle shed.

There was a strange graveyard in the foreground with dead people springing forth from the earth, resurrected, embracing each other joyfully. I copied each one, but I deliberately embellished the couple in the corner enjoying the warmest embrace. I gave the girl long dark curly hair. I gave the man a little beard with a hint of sparkly highlight on his earlobe.

I wanted Rax to look at it closely but he only gave it a quick glance every time he went to have a chat with Sarah. I hoped he'd look at it more carefully after the lesson. I was sure I understood. He was being particularly cautious. It would look strange, even suspicious, if he singled me out.

I didn't like it all the same. School was so lonely now. Rita and the other girls hissed slag at me whenever I passed. The boys made crude remarks. Toby did his best to shut them up. Then he hung back, trying to talk to me.

'I'm so sorry, Prue. I didn't mean for it to end up like this. I never thought Rita would be so mean to you. I've tried talking to her, telling her to cut it out, but she just told me to get lost.'

'Well, she would do, wouldn't she?' I said. 'And if she sees you talking to me now she'll get even meaner. You shouldn't have broken up with her, Toby.'

'But I don't reckon her any more. You're the only girl I want.'

'Oh Toby. I told you. I like you ever so much, but I don't want to be your girlfriend,' I said.

'Maybe you'll change your mind,' Toby said cheerfully.

'I don't think so,' I said, but obviously I couldn't explain why.

Rax didn't mention babysitting at all in the last art lesson of the week, but then, right at the end, when everyone else was clattering out, he asked if he could have a word with me.

'Look at her!' Rita said to her friend Aimee. 'Look at the smug little smile on the slag's face, just because old Rax wants her.'

My heart started beating fast. Rax had heard too. He paused and stood still.

'Yeah, talk about teacher's pet. *I* don't think she's that good at art, she just copies stuff,' said Aimee.

I breathed out, happy for them to carry on rubbishing my art. Toby irritatingly took it into his head to interfere.

'You shut up, you lot. You're just jealous of Prue's talent,' he said.

This naturally encouraged them to be far more vitriolic.

'Hey, you guys, how about conducting your slanging match outside in the playground?' said Rax.

'Prue *is* talented, isn't she, Rax?' Toby persisted. 'That Christmas Jesus scene is brilliant, don't you think so?'

'Yes I do,' said Rax. 'But perhaps we shouldn't keep telling Prue that or she'll get big-headed.'

'Her head's as big as an elephant's bum already,' Rita said, and flounced off, circled by Aimee, Megan and Jess.

Toby hung back, waiting for me.

'You go *on*, Toby,' I said.

He sloped off, looking miserable. I sighed. Then I looked at Rax.

'Do you really think I'm talented?' I asked.

'Yes, you're brilliant,' said Rax, but he said it flatly, as if he wasn't really engaging with the subject.

'Shall I come round usual time tonight?' I asked.

'Well. That's why I wanted a word. We won't need you to do any babysitting tonight,' he said.

He was standing at the sink, the taps full on, washing out paint pots and palettes. I wondered if I'd actually heard him properly.

'You won't need me?' I whispered. 'You've not got someone *else* to babysit, have you?'

'No, no. We're just not going out, that's all.' He stayed at the sink, splashing the palettes around, although they were all pristine.

'Why?'

'We fancied a quiet night in, watching *The West Wing* with a takeaway pizza,' said Rax.

'Oh.' I waited. He wouldn't look round. 'So. *Next* Friday then?'

Rax stood still a moment. Then he squared his shoulders. 'Maybe not, Prue,' he said. He turned round properly. His face was so tense there were lines all round his mouth. He licked his lips, wiping his hands on his jeans. 'I don't think the babysitting is really a good idea.'

'But the children *like* me. Harry loves me reading him stories, and I can always make Lily laugh. Marianne likes me too – we have all these chats together while you're getting ready.'

'I know, I know, you're great at babysitting

and my whole family adores you. But I just don't think it's a very good idea any more.'

'Why?'

'You *know* why, Prue,' he said impatiently.

'Because I love you?' I said.

'Don't!' he said, looking round anxiously, as if there were children eavesdropping in the cupboard and Miss Wilmott tape-recording at the door. He took a deep breath. 'That's why we have to stop this. It's dangerous for both of us.'

'Dangerous for you,' I said. 'You're scared you'll lose your job if anyone finds out.'

'Well, of course I am. I've got a family to support. But it's not just the job. I don't want to upset you – you're only fourteen, and you're taking our friendship so seriously.'

'Are you still trying to pretend that's all it is?'

'Yes. It's a close friendship, nothing more,' said Rax.

I started to cry.

'For heaven's sake, Prue, stop that. It's true. We haven't *done* anything.'

'Is it because I look so weird?'

'Stop it!'

'Well, *you* stop it,' I sobbed. 'I *have* to babysit, I *have* to see you. It's not the same at school, *you're* not the same. You keep on and on about my age.'

'Well, you're still a *child*.'

'If you start saying all that only-fourteen stuff again I'll start screaming.'

'Don't!' He looked alarmed, as if he thought I

189

was really going to start shrieking my head off.

'The only real time we have together is our time in the car,' I said. 'Ten minutes, once a week. That's not too much to ask, is it?'

'Twenty minutes. Sometimes half an hour.'

'What have you been doing, timing us to the exact second? "Uh-oh, I've given this girl ten and a half minutes, warning bells, she'll misinterpret my innocent caring teacherly concern as something much more serious and scary so shove her out the car quick."'

'You're being silly now,' he said, but his mouth twitched. He started laughing, shaking his head at me. 'You're a terrible girl, Prue,' he went on. 'You won't ever act the way you're supposed to. You just say whatever you think, act in the rashest way possible. Dear God, your dad must have been having a joke calling you Prudence. You're the exact opposite!'

'Well, I'm glad he didn't call me Rash. Imagine, especially if I went through a spotty stage,' I said, wiping my face with the sleeve of my sweater.

'Don't *do* that. You're worse than Harry sometimes,' he said, finding me a paper towel.

I hoped he'd wipe my eyes for me but he kept me carefully at arm's length.

'Please let me babysit tonight,' I said. 'Marianne said she was going to look out some of her clothes that are too small for her. It will look so rude of me if I don't turn up. And I told Harry I'd read him my own *Wild Things* book.

190

I was going to act it all out for him – I promised.'

'And I suppose you promised Lily you'd read her the whole of *Alice in Wonderland* and then you'd act out the Mad Hatter and the March Hare and Tweedledum and Tweedledee?' said Rax.

'Tweedledum and Tweedledee are in *Alice Through the Looking Glass*,' I said. 'There! We can have ten minutes tonight demurely discussing our favourite nursery classics. I swear I won't cry or make a scene or try to make you stay later.'

He didn't say anything.

'Don't you trust me?'

'I don't trust either of us,' he said. 'OK, OK, come round tonight. But it must be the last time. This is getting too worrying. God knows what could happen if we carry on like this. I want you to tell Marianne that you can't babysit for a while. Say you've got too much homework – any old excuse. Will you do that?'

'If you make me,' I said.

I left it at that, scared he might change his mind again. Grace was standing forlornly at the school gate. I'd forgotten all about her.

'Where have you *been*? Iggy and Figgy went home ages ago.'

'You should have gone home too, silly. I don't see why you always have to tag on to me all the time.'

'I don't see why you have to keep being so *mean* to me. I'm your *sister*. I'm not nasty to you. I keep sticking up for you when Iggy and

Figgy say stuff about you. If you must know, we've even had a little row, because they said you took Toby away from Rita on purpose, even though you didn't want him yourself – although how mad is that? – and *I* said—'

'I don't care what they said, what you said, whatever. Why can't you all just mind your own business?' I snapped, marching off.

'There you are, you're being mean again,' Grace said, hobbling after me. 'Why won't you tell me stuff, Prue? We never used to have any secrets.'

'I haven't got any secrets,' I said.

'Yes, you *have*. You act all weird and moody most of the time. You're not just playing your pretend games now, something's going on. I can tell. I think you're in love.'

'Don't be silly,' I snapped, starting to run.

'I *know* you, Prue.'

'You don't know anything,' I said, running hard.

'It's Rax!' Grace yelled after me.

Some of the kids in the street turned round and tittered.

I stood still, waiting for her to catch me up. Then I grabbed her by the shoulders, digging my fingers into her marshmallow flesh. 'Shut *up*!' I said.

'It *is* Rax,' Grace said triumphantly. 'You love him.'

'I'm warning you, Grace.'

'It's OK. Lots of girls get crushes on teachers, even funny ones like Rax,' said Grace.

'It's not a *crush*,' I said. I hated the word, with all its silly girly giggly connotations. 'It's reciprocal.'

'It's what?' said Grace.

'He loves me too.'

'Don't be daft,' said Grace, giggling.

'Don't you dare laugh at me! He *does* love me. He does, he does. He feels bad about it, he's worried about his family and his job and all that, but he can't help himself. It's as if we're made for each other, soul mates.'

Grace stared, her eyes round as marbles. Then she laughed again. 'I'm sorry! Don't – you're hurting!' she said. 'I'm not *really* laughing, Prue, it's just it's so weird. He's a teacher, he's years and years too old for you.'

'Age doesn't matter, not when you fall in love.'

'But what's going to happen?'

'Well.' I thought hard. 'Well, we'll go on seeing each other when I babysit, and then . . . and then . . .'

Grace looked at me. 'And then?' she repeated.

'We'll just have to wait and see,' I said lamely. 'I'm not going to talk about it any more. And if you breathe a word to anyone – especially Iggy and Figgy – I'll kill you, do you understand?'

I said it with such vehemence that she backed away and trailed along several paces behind me all the way home.

I knew I was treating her very badly. Part of me wanted to stop and put my arms round her and beg her to forgive me, but I still felt too angry. I couldn't bear her laughing at me, behaving as if I was making half of it up. Rax and I *were* made for each other. Fate had brought us together. We were an unlikely couple, like Jane Eyre and Mr Rochester. They belonged together. They had to wait years but their story had a happy ending.

I tried hard to look older when I got ready to go out. I wore my black sweater, and hitched my school skirt up like a miniskirt. I stuffed my feet into a pair of ancient strappy high-heeled sandals from our dressing-up box. They'd been a ten-pence jumble-sale find long ago. Grace and I used to shuffle about happily, pretending to be big ladies. They were still several sizes too big for me, but I strapped them up as tightly as they would go, determined to make myself look as sophisticated as possible. I still had to walk with a hop-skip-shuffle to keep them on my feet, but I hoped Rax wouldn't notice when he drove me home. I didn't care how many times I twisted my ankle on my way there.

Mum created a scene about the shoes. She was shocked by my painted face too. I took no notice of her.

'I don't know what to do with you, Prudence,' she wailed. 'You're getting so wilful. Just you wait till your father gets home! He'll give you such a talking to.'

I held my tongue. It was starting to look as if Dad might never recover his speech. He had abruptly lost all interest in repeating words after me. He refused to make any attempt to say anything to us, though he still swore when especially irritated. This was a great deal of the time. However, the nurses said he was improving dramatically. He had supposedly started to walk during his physiotherapy sessions but he barely turned over in bed while we were there.

Someone had put a television in his room, thinking it an act of kindness. Dad behaved as if a miniature Kingdom of Hell was flaming at the end of his bed. Whenever the nurses switched it on he pulled the sheets up over his head, as if in fear of being scorched. But as the days passed he gradually peeped at several programmes, watching with one eye. Now he gazed avidly at the screen and shushed us if we spoke during his favourite shows.

'Do you think Dad will let us have a telly when he comes home?' Grace asked eagerly.

'What are you going to buy it with, Monopoly money?' said Mum.

She was still sifting through the bills and final demands every day. She got in such a state that she plucked up the courage to ask Dad what we should do.

Dad ignored her. Mum asked again, louder, though she went pink, terrified a passing nurse might hear about our money problems.

Dad still took no notice whatsoever, though we knew there wasn't anything wrong with his hearing.

Mum didn't pursue it. She managed to make small talk and gave Dad her usual kiss on his forehead, but on the bus going home her lip started quivering.

'It's all very well for your father, tucked up safe in the hospital,' she said. 'But what are we going to do when these bailiffs come and bash down the door?'

'Can't we sell the shop, Mum?' I asked.

'It would kill your father, Prue. He loves the shop so, you know he does. And anyway, *I* can't put it on the market, it's your dad's property. I doubt if anyone would buy it now anyway. It needs so much work doing to it – and the whole parade's gone to seed.'

'So what will happen to us?' Grace asked.

'We'll manage somehow,' I said. 'If we get slung out of the shop then they'll have to rehouse us *somewhere*.'

'On the Wentworth estate!' Mum said. 'And what would we have to live on, anyway?'

'You'd get . . . I don't know, unemployment benefit?'

'Your dad's never forked out for his proper national insurance payments, or mine either,' said Mum.

'Then you'll just have to put Grace and me on the streets,' I said, joking.

'You're starting to *look* like a street girl!' Mum shouted after me now, as I went out the door. 'Whatever will your teacher think, going babysitting looking like that!'

'I look fine. You're just hopelessly old-fashioned,' I said, but I kept glancing at my reflection anxiously all the way to Laurel Grove.

Marianne answered the door to me. I saw her initial bemused expression. Then she smiled, rubbing her forehead above her nose.

'I look funny, don't I?' I said.

'What? No, no, of course not. Come on, Prue. You look very original, as always – and enviably *skinny*. No, I've just got a bit of a headache, that's all. You know, time of the month and everything.' She peered at me in the light of the hall. 'You've gone a bit mad on your make-up tonight, haven't you?'

'I *knew* I looked awful.'

'Just a bit . . . bright. Why don't you try slightly subtler shades? Which lipstick do you use?'

'I haven't *got* any lipstick, or any other make-up. I just have to use my paints.'

'I *see*. Yeah, that's a bit of a problem. Here, come up to my room, let's see if I can find you anything.'

I had to follow her upstairs and into her bedroom. She rummaged through her messy cosmetic bag.

'Hang on, I know I've got a dusky pink lipstick somewhere.'

I couldn't tell her that I'd experimented with it several times, that every time I came to babysit I couldn't stop myself creeping into their bedroom and examining everything in it. I'd even taken to lying on her pillow and pretending that Rax was lying right next to me.

I averted my eyes from their bed now and let Marianne wipe off all the paint with her make-up remover cream. She started applying her own make-up on my face.

I could hear chuckles and shouts from the children in the bathroom. I thought Rax was giving both of them a bath. I was alarmed to open my eyes after Marianne had finished shadowing them to see Rax reflected in the mirror, watching us.

'Oh, sorry!' I said foolishly. 'Shall I go and see to the children now?'

'We're not finished yet!' said Marianne. 'What about eyeliner? Just a very subtle grey shade? Keith, you haven't left the kids in the bath, have you?'

'No, no, they're in their jim-jams. I'm just looking for Harry's Honeybear, but I got distracted by the make-up session. It looks great.'

'Just call me the makeover queen,' said Marianne. She gathered my long wild hair in her hands. 'Hey, let's see what your hair looks like pinned up.'

I could feel myself blushing. I felt horribly self-conscious in front of Rax. I didn't want Marianne dabbing at me any longer, even if she was good at it.

'No, it looks silly up. I don't like it,' I said.

I liked my hair springing over my face and bouncing round my shoulders. I felt too exposed with it pinned up. But Marianne twirled it round her finger, and fixed it in a little chignon on top.

'There!' she said. 'Oh, that looks so *good*! You've got such a lovely neck, Prue, just like a little ballet dancer.'

I pulled a face, fidgeting.

'Doesn't she look lovely, Keith?' said Marianne.

'Yes, she does,' said Rax. 'But maybe you should be getting on with *your* hair and make-up, Marianne, or we'll never get out. The film starts at half past eight.'

Marianne sighed. 'We can always get it out later on DVD. I'm not sure I can be bothered, not with this headache. I don't really feel like going out at all.'

'I think we should try to make the most of tonight. It might be our last chance for a while,' said Rax.

He looked at me. I stared into the mirror at my own reflection, pretending to admire my new hairstyle.

Rax waited a moment. 'Prue isn't sure she can keep on babysitting on a regular basis,' he said.

I swallowed. 'Yes I can.'

I didn't dare look at him.

'Didn't you tell me at school that your mum isn't too happy about it?' Rax said sternly.

'Oh, she's had second thoughts.'

'Are you sure?' said Marianne. 'We've been a bit cheeky, simply commandeering you and taking you totally for granted.'

'I'm quite sure,' I said.

'Well, that's good,' said Marianne. 'Isn't it, Keith?'

Rax said nothing. I knew he was probably furious with me but I couldn't help it. He walked out of the room, ignoring both of us.

Marianne raised her eyebrows at me. 'Take no notice. He's been a bit edgy all week. Oh well, I suppose I'd better show willing and get ready. I'd much sooner stay home and play hairdressers!'

She smiled at me. I watched myself in the mirror, smiling straight back at her. I felt so wicked. I waited for the mirror to crack, for the walls to close in on me, for the carpet to slide down into a dark pit, taking me with it.

I stayed sitting on Marianne's padded stool, the two of us smiling into the mirror, as if we were posing for our portrait.

I still felt wicked when Rax and Marianne had gone out.

I made a special fuss of the children, bending over Lily's cot, holding her little chubby fist while I sang to her. I had to struggle to set my fingers free after she'd fallen fast asleep.

Harry was in a surprisingly sweet clingy mode too. I read him my old copy of *Where the Wild Things Are*. He pretended to be a little frightened so he could sit on my lap and have a cuddle. I drew him a big, stripy, wickedly-clawed Wild Thing with his children's wax crayons.

Then I made up a new *Wild Things* story about a little boy called Harry who sailed to the land where the Wild Things are, only there was no one roaring or showing their claws this time. The Wild Things bowed low to King Harry and bought him lots of presents and lay on their backs so he could tickle their fat furry tummies.

'Like this,' I said, upending Harry and tickling him.

I had to do it again and again, but he was getting sleepy now, rubbing his eyes. I began another story about the Wild Things in the dead of winter, when the snow came right up to their snouts and they all snuggled down in their cosy burrows.

'Like this,' I said, tucking Harry under his duvet. 'There you are, Baby Wild Thing. Shut your eyes and suck your claws.'

Harry giggled and sucked his fingers and fell asleep in seconds.

I stood there in the dark nursery, listening to the faint snuffle of the children sleeping. They were both treating me like their fairy godmother but I was worse than any wicked witch, intent on working my black magic on their father.

I crept into the main bedroom again and switched on the light. I looked in the mirror and a ghost image of Marianne peered back at me accusingly.

'I'm sorry,' I whispered. 'I wish you weren't so *nice* to me. I don't want to hurt you. I just can't help it. I love him so.'

I went to their double bed and buried my face in his pillow. I imagined him there beside me, his arms round me . . .

Then I heard a door, noises, Rax's voice!

I sat up, heart thudding, not sure whether I

was still daydreaming. No, there really were voices downstairs! Oh God, how could they be back already? Had I fallen asleep? I leaped off the bed, plumping Rax's pillow, smoothing the daffodil-yellow duvet, racing across the carpet. As I came out of the door Marianne was coming up the stairs and she saw me.

She frowned. 'Prue? What were you doing in our bedroom?'

'Oh Marianne, I'm sorry. I just wanted to look in your mirror again, to see my new hairstyle and make-up,' I said.

'Oh, I see! Yes, you look lovely.'

Poor Marianne looked *awful*, greasy and greeny-white.

'I've been sick,' she said, seeing me staring. 'Keith had to stop the car.'

'You poor *thing*. Do you think you've got a bug or something?'

'No, it's just the time of the month. It sometimes hits me like this. I'll be all right once I've had a good night's sleep. I was stupid to try to go out. Oh God, my *head*.' She leaned against the banisters, her eyes closed.

'Would you like me to help you into bed?' I asked timidly.

'No, no, I'll manage. Get Keith to give you your money, eh?'

'But I haven't earned it.'

'That's not your fault, love. Oh well, I'd better lie down or I'll *fall* down. See you next week then?'

'I hope so,' I said.

She waved her fingers at me and then trudged into her bedroom, sighing. I heard the springs creak on her bed within seconds.

I went downstairs slowly, my mouth dry, my tummy tense. Rax was standing in the hallway, still in his jacket.

'Marianne's gone to bed,' I said.

'Yes. Right. I'll take you home then.'

'All right.'

I followed him out of the front door, down the path, through the gate, into the car. I looked at Rax as he drove off.

'Are you cross with me?' I asked, in a very small voice.

'Yes,' he said.

I didn't dare say any more. We drove in silence. I tried to think of some way I could make everything all right again. This was our precious ten minutes together and it was ticking away. We were wasting it all.

The silence in the car was becoming unbearable. Rax seemed to think so too, because he reached out and switched on the radio. Loud pop music filled the car. Lyrics of lost love, broken promises, betrayals. Every line seemed to have significant meaning.

Rax stared straight ahead, frowning. He seemed to be concentrating hard on the traffic, although the back roads were nearly empty. We got to my street in just over five minutes. He drew up right outside the shop and switched off the engine. The love song stopped abruptly. The car was silent.

'Right,' said Rax. 'How much do we usually pay you then?'

'I don't want any money,' I said.

'Don't be silly. Let me pay you for a full night's babysitting. Here, take this.'

He took several notes from his wallet and thrust them at me.

'No!'

'Take it. It's a bit extra, to thank you for being such a good babysitter.'

'Will you let me keep coming?'

'No. I told you. This has got to stop. It's getting out of hand. I think Marianne senses something. That's maybe why she was ill.'

'No it isn't! She *likes* me, Rax, she wants me to keep coming. It's just that you won't let me.'

'Yes.' There was a very long pause. 'Well. Off you go then.'

'Is that it? You're not even going to say goodbye properly?'

'For heaven's sake, Prue, you'll see me at school often enough.'

'But it's different there. We can't talk properly. You're the teacher and I'm the pupil.'

'We *are* teacher and pupil.'

'What about if we weren't? If I didn't even go to Wentworth? How would you feel about me then?'

'I'd feel exactly the same as I do now. You're a child of fourteen.'

'The same age as Marianne when you started going out together. What if Marianne and I were both girls in your class at school? Would you like her best – or me?'

'Will you *stop* this! You're distorting everything, playing silly games. Look, Prue, I don't want to hurt you, but you must understand. I'm your schoolteacher. We could both get into such huge trouble. I took an interest in you because you were new to the school and finding it hard going and I sympathized. I tried to help you and then I made the big mistake of asking you to babysit for me and now somehow it's all become too intense, too worrying. I feel so guilty, which is mad, because nothing's actually *happened.*'

'It has now,' I said, and I reached over and kissed him on the lips.

I'd never kissed anyone properly before but I'd imagined it enough times and I'd practised how to do it on the inside of my arm. It was a timid, dry-lipped kiss – but it was a real kiss all the same.

'For God's sake!' Rax said, trying to pull away.

I kissed him again, sliding my arms round his neck and holding him tight so that he couldn't pull away from me. After a few seconds he stopped trying. He kissed me back, deeply and passionately. I was so happy I didn't care about anything or anyone any more. I just wanted to freeze time and stay inside the car, kissing Rax for ever.

'Prue, we're right outside your shop,' Rax said. 'Your mother—'

'She's not expecting me back for ages, you know that.'

But there were people coming out of the Chinese takeaway, looking in our direction.

'Oh God,' said Rax. He started up the car and we drove off.

'Where are we going?'

'I don't know. Round the block. I just need to think what to do,' he said.

I kept quiet then, peering out at the dark streets. We circled the block, but Rax didn't stop. We drove on to the outskirts of the town. We were only a mile or so away from the hospital and my dad's stroke unit. I wondered what he would say if he knew his elder daughter was driving in the dark with her schoolteacher sweetheart.

We drove down a dark lane with fields on either side, and then Rax drew up beside a clump of trees.

'Where are we?' I whispered.

'Oh, this is just . . . somewhere I used to come,' Rax said. He was whispering too.

I wondered if it was somewhere he came with Marianne. I didn't want to ask. I didn't want him to think about her. I didn't want him to think about anyone but me.

I reached over to kiss him again.

'No! No, listen, Prue, we've got to talk,' he said, trying to turn his head.

'I don't want to talk. You'll just say sensible things and I won't want to listen. Let's just do this.'

I kissed him and he kissed me back. This time I couldn't even think what it was like, or wonder who he'd kissed before. There was no one else in the world. We were whirling in our own starlit space.

'I love you,' I said breathlessly. 'I love you, I love you, I love you.'

I waited.

'Tell me you love me just a little tiny bit,' I begged.

'Prue—'

'Go on. You said it before, when you drove off that time. You said it then because you weren't sure I could see, and you could pretend it didn't really count. Say it now, Rax. Say it properly.'

'I love you.'

'Oh!'

'But this is crazy. We're both mad. You're still so young.'

'Shut *up*.'

'And I'm married, I love my family, I don't want to do anything to hurt them. I don't want to do anything to hurt *you*. You're enjoying this now because it's so exciting and romantic and dangerous. It's the best game in all the world. It's *my* imaginary game too. Don't you think I haven't lain awake at night thinking about you, wishing we could be together, fantasizing all sorts of things.'

'*Really?*'

'Of course.'

'Then why have you been trying to stop seeing me?'

'Because there is no way we can ever be together. You know that, don't you?'

'Maybe . . . maybe sometime—?'

'It's not going to happen.'

'But we love each other so much.'

'You think you love me—'

'I *do!*'

'And next year you'll fall in love with another teacher, or maybe an artist, whoever – and then at art college you'll fall passionately for the scruffiest student—'

'You really think I could go to art college?'

'And then another student, and then another, and then *eventually* you'll meet the man of your dreams and you'll live with him and have his children and then one night you'll be kissing each other and he'll ask you about your past loves and you'll say, "Oh yes, I remember when I was fourteen. I fell in love with my art teacher," and I bet you'll have a struggle to even remember my name.'

'Will you always remember *my* name?'

'Oh yes. There'll be no forgetting you, Prudence King.'

'You haven't kissed any of the other girls at school?'

'For God's sake, what do you think I am? Of course not.'

'But you're glad now that you kissed me?'

'I'm very happy, very unhappy, very confused,' he said. 'I don't know what to do now.' He let out his breath in a long sigh. 'I really don't know.'

I couldn't see his face properly in the dark. I felt it very gently with my fingers.

'I think you're looking sad. *Please* don't be sad, Rax. Be happy. *I'm* happy, the happiest I've ever been in my whole life. I never dreamed I could feel like this. I've read all sorts of books, I've pretended stuff, but I had no idea it would feel so wonderful.'

'Oh Prue. Come here.' He pulled me nearer, his arms right round me, holding me tight, my head on his chest. I was stretched sideways, bits of the car sticking into my waist and hip and leg, but I'd have happily let someone saw right through me just to stay in his arms. He very gently kissed the top of my head, nuzzling into my hair.

'It's starting to escape from the topknot already,' he said. 'Ouch, there's a hairpin! Do you mind if I take the pins out and let it hang free again? Your new hairstyle's very sophisticated, but I like it better the old way.'

I shook it free at once, combing it with my hands. Rax played with it too, winding strands round his fingers.

'I love your hair,' he said.

'It's *horrible*! I wish I had straight silky hair.'

'Your hair's like you.'

'Yes, wild and mad and untidy.'

'OK, wild, but also springy and full of life. And utterly uncontrollable. What am I going to do with you, Prue? What are we going to do?'

'I know,' I said. 'We're going to start driving and keep on driving, all through the night, until we get somewhere we've never been before, where no one knows us, and we'll start our new life together, Prue and Rax. We'll find some old cottage or beach shack, we'll live very frugally on bread and cheese – maybe chips! – and you won't go to work and I won't go to school. We'll paint all day. You'll teach me lots of things. We'll go for long walks hand in hand and in the evenings we'll curl up together and then we'll read. Maybe you'll read to me – would you like that?'

'I'd like that. I'd like all of it,' said Rax. 'If only!'

'Let's make a wish that it will come true some day,' I said. I reached up and pulled out one of my spiralling hairs.

'What are you doing?'

I found his left hand and wrapped my hair round and round his ring finger. 'There! That means that *one* day you'll be mine. I'm wishing it. You wish it too, Rax. Come on, close your eyes and *wish*.'

'Sometimes you're more like four than fourteen,' said Rax. But then he went quiet, holding onto his own hand. I knew he was wishing too.

'OK. That's the future taken care of,' he said. 'But we're still in the present now. I've got two little children and a sick wife at home. If she wakes up she'll be wondering what the hell has happened to me. *I'm* wondering. Maybe I've gone crazy. Come on, let's get you back home again.'

'It's still quite early. We could stay another half hour, easily.'

'No, it's time to go, Prue,' he said, gently pushing me back into my seat.

We drove off down the lane.

'We *could* drive up to Scotland, down to Cornwall, across to Wales—' I said.

'We could. But we're not going to. We're going to take you straight back home, OK?'

'*This* time.'

'This time,' Rax said.

'But *one* day—'

'Yes, one day,' he repeated wearily.

'Are you just humouring me?' I asked.

'Yes. And humouring myself too.'

'We'll work it all out, Rax, you'll see. I swear I won't make things difficult for you at school. I'll be the total soul of discretion. Don't laugh at me, I *will*. I'll do whatever you say, I promise, just so long as I can still see you in secret just a little bit.'

I went on burbling, fearful now because Rax had gone so quiet. But when we came to my street he parked a little way up the road, glanced round quickly and then gave me one last long wondrous kiss.

'Out you get, right now, or I really will drive off with you,' he said.

'Then I'm staying!'

'Prue. Please. Go now.'

'One more kiss?'

'What happened to your doing whatever I say?'

'OK, OK. Goodnight, darling Rax. See you at school.'

'Ssh! Yes, right. Off you go now, there's a good girl. No hanging about or waving or blowing kisses, OK?'

I got out of the car and walked obediently to the shop door without even turning round. I unlocked the door and stepped inside, into the stale, musty world of sad old books that no one wanted to read any more.

Mum was upstairs in the kitchen with all our bank statements and bills spread all over the table.

'Oh Mum, put them *away*. They'll just stop you sleeping,' I said.

Mum looked at me, red-eyed. 'I'm not sleeping whether I look at them or not,' she said. She paused, glancing at some of the crumpled bills.

'I had no idea,' she said. 'I can't work out your dad's system. I know I don't have a head for business but even I can see you need to pay your bills, you can't just let them *slide*.'

I didn't want to slide down this familiar dreary slope with Mum. I wanted to stay soaring above the stars with Rax.

'I tried to tackle your dad about it, but he was in one of his moods. He really doesn't like it

213

when you're babysitting, Prudence. I think it worries him. Well, it worries *me*, dear. It's too much responsibility for a girl your age.'

'Mum, *please*. Look, I'm tired, I'm going to bed.'

Grace was waiting for me too, asking endless questions. I took no notice, humming under my breath as I got ready for bed.

'Do you really love Rax?' she asked. 'You *do*? You are weird, Prue. What's the point? I mean, obviously he doesn't love you.'

'How do you know?' I said, before I could stop myself.

'He's married, he's got children!' said Grace.

'I know. But that doesn't stop you falling in love if the right person comes along.'

'You are so nuts!' said Grace. Then she paused. 'You don't *mean* it, do you? Prue, has he said anything? Has he told you stuff? Has he kissed you?' She started spluttering with laughter, lying back on her bed and drumming her legs in idiotic fashion.

'Stop it!' I said. 'Stop being so ridiculous!'

'Imagine kissing *Rax*!' Grace chortled. 'Oh yuck yuck yuck! That stupid beard mustn't half scratch and tickle!'

'Just shut *up*, you fat lump. I don't know why you find it so funny. No one's ever going to want to kiss *you*. You're pathetic.'

Grace stopped, as if I'd thrown a bucket of water over her. 'You're the one who's pathetic,' she said. 'You're the one everyone laughs about at school. You're the one who gets a stupid crush

214

on a manky old teacher. You're the one who pretends all sorts of stupid stuff, making out you're having this big grown-up affair when all the time I bet he's just feeling sorry for you!'

I flew at her, putting my hand over her mouth to stop her saying it. She struggled and then bit my fingers hard. I slapped her; she pulled my hair. I tried to bang her head, she kicked at me, and then we rolled off the bed with a thump.

'Girls, girls! Whatever's happening!' Mum shouted, rushing in.

We were still kicking and slapping there on the floor.

'Just you *stop* that, both of you! What are you playing at? Have you both gone demented? I need you to be grown-up sensible girls, yet here you are behaving appallingly! It's that school, isn't it? You've only been there five minutes and yet you've both changed so dreadfully. You talk so badly now, Grace, and you just giggle giggle giggle with those friends of yours on the phone. As for you, Prudence, you've become so wilful, doing exactly as you please, and you go out of here painted like a street girl. I can't bear it! I wish your father was here. Oh dear God, why can't he hurry up and get better and come *home*?'

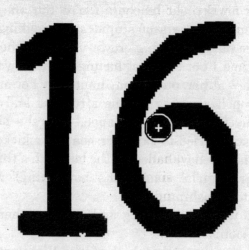

16

I wouldn't make friends with Grace. I wouldn't even talk to Mum properly, but I did mind the shop for her on Saturday morning while she went to Tesco. For a long time we had no customers whatsoever. I roamed round and round the shelves, picking up odd volumes here and there, sifting one pile of books and shunting others into corners.

Dad had always had his own idiosyncratic display system. He divided his stock into categories – fiction, biography, art, general paperbacks, juvenile, etc. – but his cheap shelving wasn't flexible, so large art books and children's picture books were over on the big shelves near his desk and little Everymans were crammed willy-nilly into odd corners. For years now newly-bought stock had simply been stuffed wherever he could find a space.

There was a special locking cabinet of supposedly precious books but he'd lost the key long ago and so he'd had to jemmy the door open. We were supposed to sit at the desk in front of the cabinet, on guard, but this was pointless. No serious collector wanted Dad's precious books. There were a couple of illustrated Rackhams but some of the colour plates were missing; then there were several sets of Dickens and the Brontës, but very faded and foxed; there were various first edition modern novels but mostly without their dust wrappers. All our books were as faded and out of fashion as our family. No wonder we had fewer and fewer customers.

I dealt with one old lady looking for a book she'd loved as a little girl, and a middle-aged man came in looking for Rupert annuals. Then a whole hour went by with no one. I flicked through an old water-stained book of favourite artists through the ages. I wanted to find someone who painted Rax-style men but didn't have much luck. He was long and lean and soulful like an El Greco, but the men were too effeminate and pop-eyed. He was pale with a pointy beard like a Veronese or a Titian, but their men were too square-shouldered and muscular. He was dark and pensive like Picasso's Blue Period men, but they were too angst-ridden and melancholy. I flicked through the book to the end and then started sketching my own Rax on the back page. I knew every feature so well it was as if he was posing in front of me. I was lovingly shading in the hollow under his cheekbones and highlighting the sweet curve of his mouth when the shop bell rang. I looked up, wondering if I could possibly have conjured him up out of sheer longing.

It was Toby.

I slammed the book shut. 'Not you again!'

'That's not very welcoming,' said Toby. He came over to the desk and touched the art book. 'Let's see.'

'No,' I said, hands tight over the edge of the pages so he couldn't open it.

'You're not supposed to draw in books,' said Toby.

'It's not worth anything, and it's my book anyway,' I said, shoving it under the desk. 'Just go *away*, Toby. I don't want to see you.'

'I'm a customer,' he said, pretending to look at the books.

'Yeah, a customer who can't read,' I muttered, but not loud enough for him to hear.

'Seriously, I want to buy a book. I'm really getting into reading now. What would you recommend?'

'Oh Toby, you've got us both into enough trouble with your wretched reading.'

'I'm sorry about Rita and the other girls. I thought they'd have stopped giving you a hard time by now.'

'I don't care.'

'I don't know what I ever saw in her. She came round to my house last night and said she was prepared to take me back.'

'Well then!'

'But I said I wasn't interested.'

'Then she'll *really* have it in for me on Monday morning.'

'We could have fun together, you and me, Prue. Just as friends, like. I could help you out in the shop, clear up all this stuff on the floor. You just tell me where you want all these boxes to go, I'll shift them for you.' He seized one as he spoke, lifting it a little too recklessly. The soft cardboard sagged and twenty-odd volumes fell out all over the dusty floor.

'Whoops!' he said.

'Careful! Honestly, Toby, will you leave them *alone.*'

'Hey, look at these!'

Toby was looking through the old volumes of Victorian pornography, his mouth an O of astonishment as he pored over the colour plates of the Reverend Knightly and his cavorting congregation.

'Where did you get these dirty books?' he said.

'They're not "dirty" books. It's Victorian erotica,' I said haughtily, though I couldn't help blushing.

'Fancy your dad selling porn!'

'It's not. All sorts of highly respectable people collect it.'

'Yeah, and you and I know why. You're such

a *weird* girl, Prue. Here's you looking at hot stuff like this as cool as a cucumber, and yet you get all fussed when I simply try to kiss you.'

I wondered what he'd think if he saw the way I kissed Rax. It all seemed so sad. There was Rita wanting Toby and Toby wanting me and me wanting Rax – but Rax wanted me back. He *did* want me, I knew he did. Though why had he seemed so unhappy last night, in spite of everything?

'Prue?' said Toby.

'What?'

'Are you all right? You look as if you've got a pain.'

'No. No, I'm fine. I just want to be on my own for a bit, Toby. You go now. Look, take one of the naughty vicar books. If anything will encourage you to read, he will. And if it gets too much of a struggle you can always look at the pictures.'

'Are you sure? I'll buy it. How much is it?'

'I haven't a clue. It isn't priced. Just take it.'

'Well, I'll just borrow it if you don't mind. Can I have a bag or something? I don't want my mum or my sisters to see it!'

Mum and Grace came into the shop while Toby was leaving. Mum looked disappointed.

'Can't you stay a bit, lad? We're just going to have a cup of tea and some shortbread. And if you can wait half an hour or so, I'm making a batch of rock cakes to take to the hospital this afternoon.'

'Do stay, Toby,' said Grace. 'Mum's rock cakes taste so yummy when they're hot out of the oven.'

So Toby stayed, holding his book bag very gingerly, as if it was burning his hands.

'What have you got there, then, Toby?' Mum asked.

Toby went scarlet. 'Oh, nothing,' he said foolishly.

'Nothing?' said Mum. 'It's one of our books, isn't it? What have you been buying?'

I waited to see what he'd say. He seemed at a total loss for words.

'Toby's a bit embarrassed about it,' I said, teasing him.

Toby looked agonized.

'It's actually an old Rupert annual. He used to love them when he was little, but he feels silly wanting a kid's comic book.'

'Oh, *sweet*,' said Grace. 'I always loved Rupert, Toby. Hey, my friend Figgy told me this great joke. What's Rupert's middle name? Can't you guess? It's "The". You know, Rupert *the* Bear.' She went into peals of laughter.

Toby laughed too, relieved. He was very kind to Grace, chuckling at joke after stupid joke. He was very polite to Mum, chomping up the last of her shortcake and then eating *three* rock cakes, rolling his eyes and kissing his fingers in a pantomime of appreciation.

I was grateful to him but irritated too. My sister's silly jokes were excruciating. My mum had simply made a batch of boring old rock cakes, for goodness' sake.

'I wish my mum made cakes,' said Toby.

'Rock cakes are very simple, lad. I'll write you out the recipe. Your mum could whip you up a batch in a jiffy.'

'My mum isn't a whipper-upper. She's a shove-it-in-the-microwave lady,' said Toby. He nodded at Grace and me. 'You're so lucky! It must be wonderful to have real home baking.'

'We *are* lucky,' said Grace, giving Mum a hug.

I felt such a pang. Why couldn't I be nice like them? Why did I always have to be so prickly and grudging and difficult?

Oh God, did I take after Dad?

'Tell you what, you ought to sell your shortbread and rock cakes in the bookshop,' said Toby. 'Yes, serve coffee and home-made cakes. They do that in bookshops now – the one down the shopping centre's got a coffee shop; it would be very popular with your customers.'

'*What* customers?' I said.

'Oh dear,' said Mum. 'Prue's right. We really don't seem to get many customers nowadays.'

'You want to advertise your books on the Internet. That's how everyone does business nowadays,' said Toby. 'I could help you set it all up. I can't really type it all out for you, I'd get the words mixed up, but Prue could do that.'

'But we haven't got a computer, Toby. They cost hundreds of pounds.'

'No probs! My eldest sister's going out with a

guy who works in this fancy office and they're forever upgrading their equipment and chucking the old stuff out. He could get hold of a perfectly good PC for you for next to nothing. Then you could surf the Net, look at e-bay, see what sort of book bargains people were offering. I bet it would make all the difference to your business.'

'Do you really think so?' Mum said, leaning forward eagerly.

'I *know* so,' said Toby, swaggering a little. 'That's how most businesses are run now. You can trade on the Internet and send the books off by post. Grace could package them all up for you, couldn't you, Grace?'

'Ooh yes, I could do. I'm good at doing parcels. And I *love* bubble wrap, it's such fun to pop,' said Grace.

'That way you'd attract a new type of customer. Then if we also tidied up the shop a bit, gave it a lick of paint, advertised your coffee and cakes, it would appeal to your traditional book buyer too.'

They were staring at him as if he was a second Moses and he had Ten Business Commandments straight from God. They *were* good ideas too. This boy who could barely read had far better ideas than I'd ever had.

'Toby's right, Mum,' I said.

Toby flicked his hair out of his eyes and gave me a huge, dazzling grin. Grace sighed. Mum sighed too.

'I know Toby's got some very good ideas,' she said. 'But what would your dad say? You know what he thinks about computers. He'd never agree to have one in the shop. I'm sure he wouldn't like the coffee and cake idea either. He'd think I was trying to turn the shop into a café.'

'You could do it while Dad's still in hospital,' I said.

'Oh Prue, I wouldn't dare,' said Mum. She paused. 'Would I?'

She went on about it after Toby went off, clutching his Victorian volume in his carrier bag. She talked about it on the bus all the way to the hospital.

'Perhaps now he'll see we have to change with the times,' she muttered. 'We could try out this computer idea, especially if we got it for almost nothing. And I could maybe ask one or two customers if they'd fancy a cup of coffee. I could try it out for free first, to see if they liked the idea. What would be the harm in that?'

'That's it, Mum, you tell Dad,' I said.

But when we got to the stroke unit Dad had something to tell *us*.

He wasn't in bed as usual. He wasn't even in his pyjamas and dressing gown. He was sitting bolt upright on one of the plastic chairs, dressed in his old suit, the one he'd been wearing when he'd had his stroke. He even had his tie neatly knotted. He clutched a notebook on his lap.

'Oh Bernard, you look wonderful, dear! Quite your old self!' said Mum.

'You look ever so smart, Dad,' said Grace.

'Hello, Dad. You really do look great,' I said.

He nodded at us all, taking his time, like a king on his throne waiting for his unruly courtiers to settle down. Mum wedged herself into another plastic chair and Grace and I perched uncomfortably on the end of the bed.

Dad cleared his throat. We sat expectantly. He raised the notebook lopsidedly, his good hand doing most of the work. He fumbled with the pages, trying to get it open at the beginning. Mum leaped up to help but he glared at her furiously, so she subsided again. Dad fiddled with the flimsy paper. I saw my own careful printing. It was my truncated version of his Magnum Opus! It hadn't got lost at all.

Dad cleared his throat once more. 'I – Bernard King – think – think – think – my – home-town – of – Kingtown – reflects – the – moral – degeneracy – of – our – current – unstable – and – unsatisfactory – age.'

He said it very slowly, without expression, struggling at each word, his mouth working as if he was chewing toffee, his eyebrows going up and down with the effort. But he *said* it, the entire sentence.

'Bravo!' said Mum, clapping him, tears pouring down her cheeks.

'Brill, Dad! Like, wow!' said Grace.

Dad winced at each word but for once let it ride. He looked at me triumphantly.

'I thought you'd thrown it away, Dad!' I said.

'Aha!' said Dad.

'You seemed totally fed up with the whole idea of reading aloud,' I said.

'With – you,' said Dad.

'So you've been secretly practising all by yourself?'

Nurse Ray put her head round the door. 'I should say so! He's been at it night and day for weeks, head in that book, mutter mutter mutter. I offered to help him but he wouldn't be having it. Wanted to teach himself, bless him.'

Dad huffed, irritated by her tone.

'Ooh, don't get shirty with me now, Bernard,' Nurse Ray said. 'You know you love me really, don't you, darling?'

Dad rocked backwards and forwards at her presumption, and she laughed at him.

'Have you told them your good news?' said Nurse Ray.

'Good news,' Dad agreed.

'It's splendid news, Bernard, seeing you reading your own book!' said Mum. 'Can you manage a bit more?'

Dad shook his head. 'Good news – going home!'

'Yes, dear, you carry on making progress like this and you'll soon be better and able to come home,' said Mum.

Dad tutted at her. 'Going home *now*,' he said. 'Today. *Now!*'

'Well, not just yet, dear. When the doctors say so,' Mum said, flustered.

Nurse Ray was nodding at her. 'He's right!

That's why we've got him all dressed up a treat in his suit. Dear God, I had to tie that tie for him three times and he still wasn't satisfied. Like I said, Bernard, you need a nice comfy sweatshirt and a pair of trackie bottoms, then you can whip them on and off in seconds.'

Dad said a very rude word to show what he thought of sweatshirts and trackies.

'He can come home right this minute?' said Mum.

'*Now!*' Dad said impatiently.

'We had a case conference yesterday and we all agreed that Bernard's more than ready to leave us,' said Nurse Ray. 'He's made that perfectly clear!'

'But he can't walk!' said Mum.

'He can stand, and shuffle a few paces with his Zimmer if he puts his mind to it. We're willing to arrange some out-patient physio-therapy – *if* His Lordship co-operates!'

Dad shook his head at this.

'But how will he get about?' Mum said weakly.

'We'll let you borrow a wheelchair from the unit, and if you get in touch with this phone number here someone will come out and assess the sort of chair Bernard will need for the future. They'll install hand supports in the bathroom and give you a commode if necessary.'

'*Not!*' said Dad. 'Right. Home. Now.'

He looked at us. His eyes swivelled from Mum to Grace to me. He breathed more quickly, his mouth working. 'Not want me?' he said.

'Oh Bernard, of *course* we want you back! It's just such a shock. But it's lovely, a lovely surprise,' Mum burbled.

Grace and I were still so stunned we couldn't say a word.

'I've got Bernard's bag all packed, and he's got all the medication he needs for the next few weeks. Make sure he takes his Warfarin.'

'Rat poison!' said Dad.

'Yes, but you're not a rat, darling, and it's thinning your blood nicely so you don't have another stroke,' said Nurse Ray, putting her arm round him. 'I shall miss your grumpy little ways, Sugar Lump!' She gave him a big kiss on his whiskery cheek.

Dad huffed again, but he patted her with his good hand.

Then we had to get him home.

'Will the ambulance men come and collect us?' said Mum.

'No dear, we can't spare an ambulance. Can't you take him in your car?'

'We haven't *got* a car,' said Mum. 'We can't take my husband on the *bus*!'

We had to call a minicab and manoeuvre Dad into the front, Mum and me heaving him onto the seat and tucking his legs in, while he snapped at us impatiently. Then Mum squeezed into the back seat, Grace and me squashed in beside her, with the wheelchair collapsed in the boot.

It cost £11.50 to get home. Mum could only

just scrape up enough money from her purse, and the cab driver had to do without a tip.

We sat Dad in the wheelchair and then struggled to get him up the step and into the shop. Dad snuffled up the stale smell of book as if the room was full of roses.

'Home now,' he said.

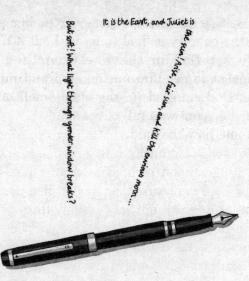

But soft! What light through yonder window breaks?

It is the East, and Juliet is

the Sun! Arise, fair sun, and kill the envious moon . . .

It was a terrible struggle getting Dad upstairs. The physiotherapist had taught him how to do it. He had to put his good foot up on the first stair, steady it, then somehow swing the bad one up beside it, balance, get his breath back, start again with his good foot up . . . Taking things one step at a time had a whole new meaning. We laboured over each step with Dad, Grace calling encouragement from the banisters, me walking backwards leading Dad up, Mum behind, her arms outstretched, ready to catch him whenever he faltered.

Dad was drenched in sweat by the time he got to the top. He insisted that he wasn't ready for bed though – he'd had enough of lying in a bed in that extremely-rude-word hospital. He was out of breath and his words were going again, but we certainly caught the gist of his meaning.

We helped him into his armchair. He sat propped up on all the cushions we could find, his feet sticking out on the leather pouffe. He looked horribly stiff and uncomfortable in his suit but he wouldn't let Mum loosen his collar and tie or even put his slippers on. He clutched my mini version of his Magnum Opus like a Bible. Every now and then he fumbled the pages open and read out a further line or two. Sometimes he simply repeated the first paragraph. Each time Mum reacted with awe and astonishment, and Grace and I clapped and commented too.

Mum made Dad a scratch supper of egg and bacon and sausage and beans and chips.

'If only I'd known you were coming home today I'd have made a special steak and kidney pud for you,' Mum said, though she had no money left in her purse. The fridge was nearly empty. The three of us went without the fry-up, making do with beans on toast.

Dad only picked at his meal, negotiating his way shakily round the plate with a fork. When he put it down he smiled at Mum. 'Lovely grub!' he said.

Mum looked so happy she made me want to cry. Dad was now so tired he could barely hold his head up. He conceded that he might be ready for a lie-down now.

It took almost an hour for Mum to help him

to the bathroom, get him undressed and into his pyjamas and lying down with a hot-water bottle. Grace and I weren't allowed to help during most of this performance, but we were summoned into the bedroom to say goodnight to Dad.

He looked much smaller in bed. Even his pyjamas seemed too big for him now, the sleeves flapping round his bony wrists. He nodded at Grace and me, and then held his cheek sideways in an oddly stiff way. We stood still for a moment, puzzled. Then Grace realized. She rushed forward and gave Dad a big kiss on the proffered cheek.

'Welcome home, Dad,' she said.

'Good girl, good girl,' he said.

I pecked at his cheek too.

'Good girl, good girl,' he repeated. 'Good – to – be – home,' he added, and then he closed his eyes.

We tiptoed back into the living room. The three of us slumped in silence, wondering what on earth was going to happen now.

Dad's docile good humour didn't last. He woke early on Sunday and had the three of us running round all day long. He insisted that we help him all the way downstairs to the shop and then got in a state because a few books had been moved around. He imagined some were missing, remembering books from years ago, insisting that someone had stolen them out of the cabinet. He bashed at the broken lock as if it had happened yesterday and swore at Mum as if she was personally responsible.

'Useless! Useless!' he screeched at her.

She cooked him another fry-up for his lunch but this time he frowned at his plate, his good hand tipping it.

'What's this?' he said.

'It's one of my special mixed grills, Bernard,' said Mum.

Dad sighed. 'Sunday! Where's . . . where's . . . ?' It took him two minutes of struggling and thumping, the egg and bacon congealing on his plate. 'My – roast – beef – and – Yorkshire!' he said in a rush.

Mum sighed too. 'Bernard, we haven't been able to afford roast beef for years, you know that. I'm sorry, I wish I could have made you a pie or a casserole, but I'm a bit short of housekeeping money just now.'

'Useless! Useless!' said Dad, as if poor Mum had been frittering it away on champagne and caviar.

'Mum *isn't* useless, Dad,' I said. 'She's done her very best since you've been ill, but we've got hardly any money left. There are all these scary letters saying they're going to send the bailiffs in. We're going to have to do something, work out a plan.'

'Rubbish!' said Dad.

'I'll show you the letters, Dad.'

'Let your dad eat his dinner first, Prudence,' said Mum.

'Don't want it,' Dad said petulantly, pushing his plate away.

'Then let *us* eat it. We're all starving hungry,' I said.

Dad glared at my impudence. I showed him the sheaf of threatening letters. He held them at arm's length, barely glancing at them.

'Rubbish,' he repeated, and then he tried to tear them up. Luckily he was too fumbly to do more than rip the edge and crumple them. Mum gathered them all up anxiously.

'We can't just tear them up, Bernard,' she said. 'Prue's right, we can't just ignore things. We need a plan.'

'Rubbish!' said Dad. He said it again and again, embellishing it with his favourite swearword. Mum tried to soothe him but he told her she was useless.

When we'd finally got him to bed that evening we were all exhausted. We hadn't dared bring up the most important thing of all – school.

'You should have let me tell him, Mum,' I said.

'But he was in such a dreadful state. He simply couldn't have borne it. I wonder if he's in a lot of pain with his bad arm and leg. Maybe that's why he's been so bad-tempered,' said Mum.

'You don't get pain if you have a stroke. His affected limbs just feel heavy, I'm sure.'

'Still, it must be awful for him,' Mum said.

'It's awful for *us*,' I said.

'What do you think he's going to say about school?' Grace said anxiously.

The phone had gone twice today, one call from Figgy, one call from Iggy, but Mum had run to the phone and said Grace was too busy to talk.

'He's not going to like it, not at all, especially when he realizes it's Wentworth. He'll be so angry with me,' Mum said. 'But what was I to do? I couldn't risk getting prosecuted. What if they'd taken you girls into care? I never wanted you to end up at Wentworth, I tried going to Kingtown High, but they've got two hundred already on their waiting lists. Oh Prue, help me make your dad understand. Maybe you could say it was all your idea? Then he might accept it more willingly.'

'OK. But I don't think he's going to accept it at all,' I said.

'But we will keep going, won't we?' said Grace. She pushed her hair back behind her ears, her chin jutting in the air. 'We *have* to keep going to Wentworth, Mum.'

'Do you really like it there, chickie?' said Mum.

'Well . . . it's OK. The lessons aren't quite as hard as I thought, and some of the teachers are kind. But it's Iggy and Figgy. They're my *friends*.' Grace's blue eyes filled with tears. 'I've never had *proper* friends before. They're just like the bestest friends in all the world. I couldn't bear it if I couldn't see them any more.'

Mum patted her hand comfortingly. 'What about you, Prudence? I expect you feel the same way about Toby.'

'Well . . .' I couldn't stop Mum thinking Toby

was my boyfriend. 'I *have* to stay at Wentworth too, Mum. I know you think it's had a bad effect on me but I know I'd argue back anyway, whether I went to Wentworth or not.'

'I know you're very good at arguing,' said Mum. 'I worry about you, Prue. I've no idea what goes on in that head of yours. I just want you to be happy, dear. If staying at Wentworth makes you happy then let's hope your dad sees reason.'

We all hoped Dad would sleep late so that Grace and I could be off and out before he started shouting for attention. We'd heard poor Mum getting up with him to help him shuffle to the bathroom at least three times in the night. But at half past seven he demanded another trip to the bathroom – and then asked to be bathed.

'Can't it wait till later, dear? The girls will need to use the bathroom soon.'

'Girls – can – wait!'

Grace and I had to go and use the dank outside loo in the back yard and then wash ourselves as best we could at the kitchen sink.

'Let's make a dash for school now,' I said. 'We'll get ourselves a sandwich and just clear off.'

We weren't quick enough. There was a commotion from upstairs. Dad had slipped getting out of the bath, and Mum couldn't get him up by herself.

'Girls! Girls, come here quickly!' she called.

'Pretend we haven't heard. We can still make a run for it,' I said.

'But what if Mum can't budge Dad? He can't stay on the bathroom floor all day,' said Grace.

'OK, OK.'

We trudged upstairs. Mum was grappling with Dad. He'd wound a towel round himself like a nappy. He was trying to preserve his dignity but it made him look like a giant baby.

'Come on then, Dad,' I said, seizing him under the arms.

Mum hauled at his bottom half and Grace pushed and pulled at his midriff. Between us we got him to his feet, and then Mum wrapped his old plaid dressing gown round him.

'Phew! What a . . . what a . . . *performance*,' said Dad as if it was all our fault. He breathed heavily, trying to compose himself.

'Sit down a minute, Bernard,' said Mum, steering him to the loo. She closed the seat and pushed him onto it.

'I'm fine, I'm fine,' he said, but he slumped sideways, his chin on his chest.

I caught Grace by the wrist and started tugging her out of the bathroom as unobtrusively as possible. Dad looked up.

'You girls – early birds!' he said.

Then he focused on our clothes. He blinked. 'Green?' he said. He looked at me, he looked at Grace. 'Peas in pod!'

Grace giggled nervously. Mum sat down heavily on the edge of the bath. I stood still. We didn't say anything – but he suddenly got it.

'School!' he said. He said it softly first. Then

he drew breath. 'School? *School?* SCHOOL!' He was bellowing now, sweat standing out on his forehead.

'Oh Bernard, calm down! You know it's not good for you to get so worked up,' said Mum. She tried to mop his brow with a flannel but he batted her away. He was trembling with fury.

'School?'

'I had to send them, dear. They were threatening us with prosecution, you know that. I didn't have any alternative.'

'Rubbish!' said Dad. He was squinting at the motif on my blazer. 'Wentworth,' he read, rolling his eyes. '*Wentworth!*'

'I couldn't get them in anywhere else, Bernard. I tried, I really did. I went to see the head at Kingtown but there's a very long waiting list. Wentworth was the only school with vacancies. It's not as bad as you'd think. There's a new headmistress, she's making all sorts of improvements.'

'Wentworth!' said Dad in disgust. He struggled to get up from the toilet.

'Careful, dear,' said Mum, trying to help.

'No! No, *traitor!*' Dad said. 'Girls! *No* school! No no no school.'

I looked at Grace. She started sobbing.

'*Please*, Dad,' she said. 'I *love* school. I have these two friends Iggy and Figgy.'

'Stupid,' said Dad.

'No, they're not stupid, they're very special,' Grace said bravely.

238

'*You're* stupid! Useless, useless, useless,' said Dad.

Then he turned to me. 'Your fault! Liar! Thief! Tart! Useless. Rubbish daughters!'

'They're not rubbish daughters! Don't say such terrible things! They're dear good girls. I won't have you hurt them like this!' Mum cried. She turned to us. 'Take no notice of your father. Go to school, girls. Quick, off you go!'

We stared at Mum. We couldn't have been more shocked if the taps or the toilet had spoken. But there wasn't time to wonder. I grabbed Grace and we ran for it. We went on running right out of the house, down the road, all the way to Wentworth.

Grace saw Iggy and Figgy in the playground and shot across to them. I saw her talking to them, waving her arms wildly. Then they hugged her, first Figgy, then Iggy. I felt ashamed. They were sweet girls in spite of their silly nicknames. They obviously really liked my sister. I wished some of the girls in my class liked me.

I had to see Rax urgently. We didn't have art on Mondays. I couldn't possibly wait till Tuesday. I didn't even know if we'd be able to get away from Dad again. And what was going to happen about Friday nights?

I hurtled across the playground, making for the art block. I knew Rax generally didn't arrive at school until later, but I was so desperate to tell him that I went looking for him just in case.

I heard Toby call out to me as I ran but I took no notice.

'Toby wants you,' said Sarah, who was bouncing a red ball on a string. She had no idea what she was doing. The ball bounced wildly backwards and forwards. Sarah cackled with laughter, making no attempt to catch it or jump it or control it in any way. It was enough for her just to watch it.

'Yes, but I don't want Toby,' I said.

Sarah blinked at me, trying to work out my meaning. I hurried past her.

'Toby *wants* you,' she called after me.

'Well, tell Toby I'll catch up with him later,' I said, and rushed on.

I chanted inside my head. *Let Rax be there, please please let Rax be there. I'll do anything, but let Rax be in his art room, all alone, so I can talk to him.*

I got to the art room, I opened the door – and wonder of wonders, Rax was sitting on his desk, shoulders slumped, staring into space.

'Rax, Rax, Rax!' I called.

He stared at me and then jumped down from his desk. 'What's the matter, Prue?'

'Oh, Rax,' I said, starting to cry.

'What is it? What's happened? Tell me!' said Rax.

'It's Dad! He knows!' I sobbed.

'What?' said Rax. He looked horrified. 'What do you mean, he knows? You didn't *tell* him, did you, Prue? What did you *say?*'

'I didn't say anything! He came home this weekend, he's getting better, he can talk now, and he saw us in our Wentworth uniform, and he says we can't come to school any more!' I wailed.

'What about you and me? Did you tell him about us?'

'Of course I didn't!'

'Oh, thank Christ.'

'But don't you see, Rax, he hates the whole idea of Wentworth. He positively forbade Grace and me to come today. We just rushed out, but he's so fierce, he won't let us get away tomorrow, and he won't let me babysit, I know he won't.'

I looked at Rax, tears streaming down my cheeks. He breathed out, leaning against his desk. I saw the look of relief on his face. I saw it and I couldn't bear it. I sobbed harder.

'Prue! Prue, stop it. Come on, calm down. It'll be all right. Don't worry. Don't cry so. You're getting in such a state over nothing.'

'Nothing! Is that all our love means to you? *Nothing?*'

'Ssh now! Of course not. But there's no point getting hysterical. We'll get everything sorted out. I'm sure you'll be able to stay at school. Prue, *please* don't cry like that.' He took two steps forward, hands outstretched, and I fell into his arms.

I wept against his chest. He patted my back like a father. 'There there,' he murmured, as if I was Harry's age. I wept harder, hating him for not caring more, but loving him because he was still my true love and soul-mate.

'I *love* you, Rax,' I said – as the art-room door swung open behind us.

We wheeled round, Rax pushing me away from him. We looked at the door. It was only Sarah, smiling at us, her red ball dangling on the end of its elastic.

Rax rubbed his forehead with the palm of his hand. Then he forced a smile on his face. 'Hello, Sarah,' he said.

'Hello, Rax,' she said cheerfully. 'Look at my red ball!'

'Great,' he said.

'Prue, Toby wants you,' Sarah insisted.

'Never *mind*,' I said, scrubbing at my eyes with the back of my hand.

'You're crying,' said Sarah.

'No, no, she's just got something in her eye,' said Rax. 'Prue, you'd better go and find out what Toby wants.'

'But I have to talk to you!'

'*I* like talking to Rax,' said Sarah.

'And I like talking to you, Sarah,' said Rax.

Sarah smiled at me triumphantly. 'You go and find Toby,' she said.

'But I *must* talk to you, Rax!' I said desperately.

'Later,' said Rax. 'Off you go now.'

I was summarily dismissed. I floundered across the playground, still crying.

'Prue, *there* you are! What's the matter?

What's happened? Is it Rita? What's she done now?' Toby said, rushing up to me.

'Nothing,' I said. 'Just leave me be, Toby.'

'But I've got the most amazing thing to tell you!' said Toby. 'Didn't you hear me shouting at you? You know that book you lent me? You'll never guess what!'

I could guess, all right. He'd read a whole page himself, or maybe a whole chapter. I didn't care if he'd read the whole book.

'I'm sorry, Toby, not now. For God's sake, can't you leave me *alone*!'

I ran away from him into school. I hid in the girls' cloakrooms until the bell went for lessons. It was English first. Mrs Godfrey was irritably teaching the balcony scene from *Romeo and Juliet*. The class read out line after line, talking like metronomes, ruining the romance and the poetry.

I ached to read Juliet but I knew Mrs Godfrey would never pick me. She was talking about the concept of love now, getting impatient when some of the class started whistling and making crass remarks.

'For heaven's sake, stop all this nonsense!' she said. 'Romeo and Juliet are one of the most famous pairs of lovers in literature. Can anyone think of a modern equivalent?'

'Posh and Becks, miss?'

'Brad and Jennifer.'

'Richard and Judy.'

'Prue and Toby,' said Rita furiously.

'No,' said Sarah. 'Prue and Rax.'

I sat very still, praying that people would keep on shouting out stupid suggestions. But Sarah had a loud voice and silenced everyone else.

'Prue and *Rax*?' said Rita.

'Yes, they're dead romantic,' said Sarah.

'Don't be silly, Sarah,' said Mrs Godfrey, sighing.

'I'm not silly,' said Sarah, getting worked up.

'No, I know, I simply meant your *suggestion* was silly,' said Mrs Godfrey.

'Prue and Rax are lovers,' Sarah insisted.

Someone gasped, someone giggled.

'Will you stop staying that, please, Sarah,' said Mrs Godfrey.

'They are, they are. Rax was hugging Prue and she said "I love you" to him,' said Sarah. 'You *did*, didn't you, Prue?'

There were more gasps. Everyone stared at me. The kids in front swivelled right round. Mrs Godfrey stood still, shocked into silence.

The bones in my spine juddered all the way down my back, as if I'd fallen from a great height.

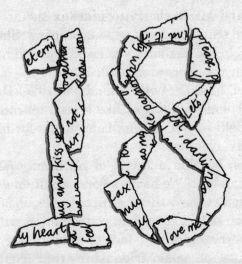

Mrs Godfrey said nothing at all to me, but she must have spoken to Miss Wilmott after the lesson. Sarah was sent for. Then me.

I'd rehearsed a dozen different excuses, stories, lies . . . but as soon as I saw Miss Wilmott's face I knew it was pointless. She looked at me with disdain, breathing shallowly as if I'd started to smell.

'I want you to tell me all about your friendship with Mr Raxberry,' she said.

My mouth dried. 'There's nothing to tell,' I mumbled. 'I know Sarah said stuff in the English lesson, but she's got it all wrong because – because she's simple.'

'Sarah might not be the brightest girl in the class, I know. That's the point. She's not the sort of girl who would fantasize. She says she saw you and Mr Raxberry together in the art room before school and you were embracing. She says you told Mr Raxberry you loved him and he held you in his arms and fondled you.'

'No!' I said. '*Fondle* sounds horrible. He was just being *kind* to me, like a good teacher.'

'I believe you've been babysitting for him on Friday evenings?'

'Yes, but I'm a friend of his family. There's nothing in it. We haven't done anything *wrong*.'

'I'm not sure that's entirely true, Prudence. I've already had a long conversation with Mr Raxberry himself. I feel that there are some aspects of your friendship that could be considered inappropriate.'

'No! No, he's done *nothing*. You mustn't blame him. All right, I *did* say I loved him, but he didn't encourage me in any way. He was just comforting me because I'm so unhappy. My father doesn't want me to come to Wentworth any more.'

Miss Wilmott leaned forward, propping her chin on her fingertips. 'Do you really *want* to stay at Wentworth, Prudence? I don't think you've made much of an effort to fit in. You are obviously gifted in certain areas, and I'm sure in good time you'll learn to cope with maths, but I haven't been at all happy with your attitude. You don't seem to understand how to behave in school. I've heard tales of unsuitable underwear and then a silly romance with one of the boys in your class. I feel that in the space of a few short weeks you've made rather a bad name for yourself.'

I felt my face flaming. 'That's incredibly unfair! I don't know who's been telling you tales, but you've got an entirely slanted viewpoint. You shouldn't be influenced by rumours and tattletales.'

'This is precisely what I mean, Prudence. I don't know whether you intend to be deliberately insolent but you certainly come across as an unpleasantly opinionated and arrogant girl. Your sister seems to be a sweet child and she's settled down well at Wentworth. I shall be happy to keep her here, but I can't help feeling that you'll be much better off elsewhere. I shall try hard to engineer a suitable transfer to another school.'

'But I *want* to stay here.'

'Why is that? Let me make myself clear. I can't risk having you and Mr Raxberry at the same school, whatever the ins and outs of your friendship. Things have to be nipped in the bud immediately. If you won't leave then I shall have to ensure Mr Raxberry finds another position.'

'No, you can't do that! He's a brilliant teacher.'

'You should have thought of that before you started acting in this ridiculous and precocious manner. If I were another kind of headteacher I would have Mr Raxberry instantly suspended. There could even be a court case. He would not only lose his job, he could find himself in very serious trouble. Did you ever stop to think about that?'

I couldn't help crying then, though I hated breaking down in front of her. 'Please don't get him into trouble, Miss Wilmott,' I begged. 'None of this was his fault.'

'I'm inclined to believe you, Prudence. So what are we going to do? Are you going to let me transfer you to another school?'

I sat there, agonized. I so wanted to save darling Rax – and yet why hadn't he wanted to save *me*? Had he told Miss Wilmott it was all my fault, that I'd got a ridiculous crush on him, that I'd made ludicrous advances to him? I burned at the thought. I wanted to tell this horrible, patronizing woman how hungrily he'd kissed me, but I couldn't do it. I loved him. I had to help him.

'All right. I'll leave Wentworth,' I whispered.

'That's very sensible of you, Prudence. Right. I'll send you to the Success Maker for the rest of the day. Make the most of your last maths tuition! The tutor in charge will tell you when you may go home. Before too long you should be notified about a new school. Off you go now. Of course I need hardly add that I'm strictly forbidding you to get in contact with Mr Raxberry from now on.'

I knew I couldn't risk running straight to Rax. I couldn't get him into any more trouble. I spent a terrible endless time in the Success Maker, in such a state of anxiety I was even more hopeless than usual, and the tutor despaired.

Sarah was part of our small dunce tuition

group. She blinked at me nervously. 'Did I get you into trouble?' she asked.

'Yes.'

'I didn't mean to. Miss Wilmott kept asking me stuff.' Sarah was nearly in tears. 'Why is it bad to love Rax, Prue? *I* love him.'

'It's not bad. Take no notice. Miss Wilmott's just being horrible.'

'Was she very cross with you?'

'Yes.'

'But you don't have to stand outside her door as a punishment?'

'She's not letting me come back to the school after today.'

Sarah blinked again, her blue eyes watering. 'Is it all my fault?' she asked.

'No,' I said, with an effort.

'It *is*,' Sarah said, her face crumpling.

'No. Don't cry, Sarah. It's OK. I don't *want* to come to this crummy old school. I hate it.'

I *did* hate it, but it felt dreadful to be excluded all the same. They kept me back an extra ten minutes by myself in the Success Maker. I realized it was so I couldn't see any of the others in my form. They were acting as if I might contaminate them. I couldn't even say goodbye to Toby.

When they eventually let me out I marched across the playground with my head held high in case Miss Wilmott or any of the staff were spying on me from their windows. Grace was hopping up and down at the gate.

'What's going on, Prue? I asked some of the girls in your class if they'd seen you and they said you were in dead serious trouble but they wouldn't say why.'

'I can't come back to Wentworth,' I said.

'Yes we can. Mum will maybe talk Dad round. Or we can just run out like we did today. We have to keep coming to school. I'd die if I couldn't stay friends with Iggy and Figgy.'

'No, Grace. You don't understand. You can keep coming to school if you can get past Dad. *I* can't. Miss Wilmott told me I can't come back.'

'What? For the whole week? What have you *done*?'

'I can't ever come back. Well, to hell with her, to hell with all of them.' I tore open my bag and pulled out all my school textbooks and exercise books. 'I won't need this – or this – or this!' I started hurling them over the wall, into the empty playground. They flew through the air like large awkward birds, pages flapping.

'Prue! Stop it! You've gone crazy. Tell me why you can't come back,' Grace said, tugging at me.

'Because I love Rax,' I said, running off down the road. I ran and ran, with Grace thudding along behind me. I rushed round the corner – and there was Rax's car. He was parked, waiting for me. He leaned out of his window. He looked very pale, but he nodded pleasantly to Grace.

'Hello, Grace. Do you think you could go home by yourself just this once? I need to talk to Prue.'

Grace stared, open-mouthed.

'Yes, you go home, Grace,' I said, and I got in the car with Rax.

We drove off quickly.

'We're not supposed to see each other any more,' I said.

'I know.'

'If Miss Wilmott saw—'

'She can't see round corners.'

'So where are we going?'

'I don't know. I don't care. I just had to see you. What's happening? Are they excluding you?'

'Miss Wilmott doesn't want me back at all.'

'Oh God. Prue, I'm so so sorry.'

'It's not your fault.'

'Yes it is. I hate myself. I let her think the worst of you, the best of me, just to save my own skin. I said it was ridiculous talking about a love affair between us. I said you simply had a crush on me, and that I was just trying to be kind.'

'Well. That's what you said before, to me.'

'And you were brave enough to stand up to me and force me to acknowledge the truth.'

'Which is?'

He hesitated. Then he said it, very softly. 'I love you.'

'You *really* do?'

'That's why I had to take a risk and see you this one last time. I didn't want you to think I didn't care.'

'Then let's keep driving. Let's really run away, you and me. I don't care where we go. We'll find a little seaside town with a harbour and boats, just like the one you painted when you were little, and we'll both eat ice creams every day.'

'I can't, Prue. You know I can't. I'm going to stay with my family, stick with my job, do all the safe sensible things. But every night when I close my eyes I'll think of us together in this car and how badly I *wanted* to drive off with you. I'll imagine us walking hand in hand at the water's edge—'

'I'll imagine it too. I'm good at pretending.'

'You've got your whole life in front of you. You won't have to pretend, you can live it for real.'

'Can we at least drive to that secret place where we kissed?'

'No. We can't go there, it would be crazy.'

'Please, Rax.'

'No. Stop it.'

'I can't bear the thought of not seeing you.'

'Listen. I told you, one day someone will ask you about the first time you fell in love and I bet you you'll struggle to remember my name.'

'I'll always remember you, and every little thing about you.'

'You wait and see. Now, I think I'd better take you home.'

'No!'

'If you arrive long after Grace your parents will think it strange.'

'I don't care. I'm in enough trouble as it is.'

'What do you think they'll say when you tell them you can't go back to Wentworth? I wish I wasn't such a coward. I ought to go and meet them and try to explain.'

'To my *dad*? Don't be silly, Rax. Listen, couldn't we meet up sometimes, after you've finished school?'

'No.'

'We would be very careful.'

'We'd still be found out sooner or later.'

'Then can't I phone you? Or write to you? *Please*, Rax.'

'No. This is it, Prue. We have to say goodbye.'

He drove me home. He did park a few metres away from the shop, but there were people wandering up and down the pavement and it was still daylight. Even I could see we couldn't kiss properly. Rax reached for my hand instead, squeezed it gently and then whispered, 'Goodbye.'

I whispered it too, and then I got out of the car and watched as he drove off. I stayed staring down the road long after he'd gone round the corner. Then I turned and stared at the shop. I looked at the uninviting window display of yellowing books in bad bindings. I stared at the peeling olive paint on the shop door and the OPEN notice hanging lopsidedly in the window panel. I couldn't stand the thought of going through that door, back into my own life.

Maybe I could run away by myself? I could make for the seaside, lie about my age, get some sort of job in a shop or a café or a hotel. I could walk along the sands every day. It would be desperately lonely but I could think about Rax, pretend he was with me, imagine our life together . . .

I started to walk down the street. Then I stopped. I couldn't *really* run away. I couldn't do it to Grace or Mum. They would be frantic if I disappeared. I didn't know about Dad. He didn't seem to want me as his daughter any more.

I took a deep deep breath as if I was about to dive into a murky swimming pool, and then opened the shop door. Grace was sitting at the desk, building copper and silver and gold towers out of the money in the till. They were very *small* towers. She saw me, and the towers tumbled down, small change spilling off the desk and rolling all over the floor.

'Oh Prue, you're back! Thank goodness! I was scared you might run away with Rax,' said Grace, rushing over and hugging me.

'I wish,' I said sadly.

'I couldn't believe it when you just hopped in his car and drove off. So are you and Rax – you know – like, really in love?'

'Ssh, Grace,' I said, looking upwards.

I could hear Mum's heavy footsteps upstairs in the kitchen.

'It's OK. I told Mum you had to stay behind and see one of the teachers. I'd never tell on you. Prue, Mum and Dad are acting kind of *weird*.'

'So what's new?' I said.

I expected Mum to be tearful and repentant

after standing up to Dad this morning. I thought he would still be apoplectic, ranting and raving in his new staccato voice. But the kitchen seemed strangely silent, though a wonderful sweet syrupy smell started wafting downstairs.

'Oh yum! Mum's baking!' said Grace. 'What do you think she's making? Jam tarts? No, I think it's treacle tart! Oh, I've got to go and see.'

She went rushing upstairs. I stayed in the shop by myself. I found the big art book and looked at my portrait of Rax on the back page. I bent over it, my finger stroking every pencilled line.

'Prue!' Grace came galloping down again. 'It *is* treacle tart, yippee. Mum says we can shut the shop early and come and have some tea.'

The kitchen was warm from the oven and thick with the smell of the golden tart shining like a sun in the middle of the kitchen table.

Dad was pushed up to the table in his wheelchair. He was sitting painfully upright, head held high, as if he was attempting to show he wasn't permanently disabled, that he could leap out of the wheelchair in one bound if he put his mind to it. He saw me, he saw Grace, but his eyes slid straight past us, as if we were invisible. He had obviously decided we were no longer anything to do with him. He took no notice of his wife either. He sat in stony isolation, his amended Magnum Opus balanced on his bony knee.

Mum was making a pot of tea. She was very

pink in the face, wearing her red-and-white checked apron, a cousin of my dreaded dress. Her hair stood out in wisps, there was a smear of flour on her nose, and the sash of her apron emphasized her thick waist – but she looked better than usual. She didn't look defeated any more.

'Hello, girls.' She looked at me. 'Are you all right, Prudence?'

I shrugged.

'Come and have a nice cup of tea.'

'Can we have the treacle tart now, Mum?' Grace begged.

'Of course, dear.'

Mum cut her a generous slice. She cut one for me too.

'I'm not really hungry, Mum.'

'You're mad! I'll have Prue's slice too, Mum. Oh, you make such *superb* treacle tarts,' Grace said indistinctly, spraying crumbs everywhere.

'I'll have to show you how to make tarts yourself sometime.'

'I'd sooner just eat yours! Are you going to serve cakes in the shop, Mum, like Toby suggested?' said Grace. Then she looked anxiously at Dad.

Mum glanced at him too. 'I don't see why not,' she said. 'I think it's a very good idea.'

Dad muttered his favourite worst word, staring straight ahead.

'Please don't swear in front of the girls, Bernard. Or me, for that matter.'

Dad swore more forcefully.

'Your dad and I have had a little tiff, girls,' said Mum. 'Come on, Bernard, there's no point sulking. You'll have a piece of my treacle tart, won't you?'

Dad clamped his mouth together as if she was about to force-feed him.

'Don't be like that,' said Mum. She paused, standing behind him. She raised her eyebrows at us, her hands resting on the handles of his wheelchair. She looked at the corner, as if she was going to wheel Dad into it and leave him there.

Grace giggled nervously.

'Useless!' Dad muttered.

'Stop it!' said Mum. 'I told you, Bernard, I'm not standing for it. You're not going to say these dreadful things to the girls. I know you're their father – but I'm their *mother*. You're upset because they're going to school but there's simply no alternative. You can't teach them now, you know you can't. And they've settled down so happily at Wentworth. Well, Grace certainly has. It's not been so easy for Prue, though she's doing really well in art.'

That was it. That was my chance. I cleared my throat.

'Mum. Dad. I've got to tell you something.'

Grace stared at me, almost dropping her slice of treacle tart. 'Don't talk about Rax!' she mouthed at me.

I shook my head at her. 'I don't really want

to stay at Wentworth,' I said. 'I'm not going any more.'

'Oh Prudence! Make your mind up!' said Mum.

'I just don't fit in there,' I said. 'Grace has got her friends.'

'You've got Toby,' said Mum.

'He's about the only one that likes me. Maybe it's my fault, I don't know. But can't I just stay home now? I can help out in the shop. I can help look after Dad.'

'Don't need – blooming looking after!' Dad said, but he reached out with his good hand and took hold of mine, squeezing it awkwardly. He thought I was being loyal to him, doing what he wanted after all. 'We can work – on Magnum Opus,' he said.

Each word was like a hammer blow but I was past caring. I just nodded weakly. I hated Dad's dry clasp. I wanted to keep the feel of Rax's hand on mine. But Dad hung onto my hand, tugging a little.

'Who's – Toby?' he asked suspiciously.

'He's a lovely lad,' said Mum – and at that moment the shop bell rang downstairs. 'We're closed!' she said. 'Wouldn't you know it! No customers all day long, and then they come calling the minute you close. Run down and see who it is, Grace.'

Grace ran. She came back two minutes later with Toby. Mum looked a little anxiously at Dad, but smiled at Toby all the same.

'Why, Toby, what a lovely surprise! We were

just talking about you, dear. Bernard, this is Toby, Prue's friend.'

Dad glared at him, still hanging onto my hand. 'How – do – you – do?' he barked.

His hand grew hot and I could feel him shaking. I suddenly realized how much effort it took for him to say the simplest thing now.

'How do you do, Mr King,' said Toby politely.

'Would you like some treacle tart, dear?' said Mum.

'Yes please!' said Toby.

'What are you doing here?' I asked, frowning at him.

'I had to see you. You wouldn't listen to me at school! It's about the book.' Toby started delving into a carrier bag and unpeeling bubble wrap.

'Which book?' I said.

'This one!' said Toby, suddenly exposing *The Intimate Adventures of the Very Reverend Knightly*.

'Toby! Put it away!' I said sharply.

'What's this book?' said Mum.

Dad dropped my hand. He waved his good arm wildly. The sweat stood out on his forehead. 'Not! Not!' he said, his speech deserting him again.

'Let's have a look,' said Grace, opening it. 'Oooh! It's ever so rude!'

'*Not!*' Dad insisted.

'Toby, that's not a very nice book to bring into the house,' said Mum.

'It was in your shop, Mrs King,' said Toby. 'Prue showed it to me.'

Mum gasped. So did Dad.

'The thing is, did you know it's ever so valuable?' Toby persisted, taking a big bite of treacle tart. 'I looked it up on my computer. They've got lots of these special antiquarian dirty books on this website, you wouldn't believe it.'

'You shouldn't be looking, a young lad like you,' said Mum.

'Yes, but guess how much the exact same set of books is selling for! I had to check with my sister, just in case I'd got the wrong end of the stick. Go on, *guess*.'

'A hundred pounds?' said Mum.

'Fourteen thousand pounds!' said Toby. 'Yes, truly.'

'My Lord! Imagine! And I've never even set eyes on the book before!' said Mum. 'Well, bless you for finding it for us, Toby. By rights you deserve some of the money if we sell it.'

'Oh no, Mrs King, it's all yours. I haven't done anything,' said Toby.

'Right!' said Dad. '*I* knew. I knew – worth – thousands.'

I was pretty sure Dad had had no idea it was worth a fortune, but he couldn't help crowing. There were feverish pink patches on his cheeks. His hands were shaking so badly he spilled his cup of tea down his waistcoat, but we all pretended not to notice. He ate a slice of treacle tart too, and had the grace to nod at Mum. 'Not bad,' he said.

'You're a brilliant baker, Mrs King,' said Toby. 'Maybe you ought to close down the bookshop altogether and start up a cake shop?'

'Rubbish!' said Dad. 'Books. Books *best*.'

I went down to the shop and found the other volumes of the Reverend Knightly. I looked through them carefully, turning the pages at the very edge, checking they were all first editions. I counted every colour plate. All five volumes seemed in near-fine condition.

Dad very laboriously composed a detailed description of the books, dictating it at snail speed. I wrote it out for him and sent letters to several specialist book dealers. Dad asked fifteen thousand for the five volumes but they weren't interested. So I got Toby to help me type it all out on a special antiquarian book site on the Internet. We still didn't get fifteen thousand, but managed to sell the lot for £12,500, which still seemed a huge sum.

'It's enough to pay off all the debts,' said Mum. 'It's really all because of you, Prue. You were the one who let Toby borrow the book, though it was a very *odd* thing for you to do. Did you look inside it?'

'Not properly,' I said.

'Hmm!' said Mum. 'Still, I suppose it's a case of all's well that ends well.' She chucked me gently under the chin. 'Cheer up, chickie. I'm so glad that you and Toby are friends. He's such a lovely boy – and he has such good ideas! He's made such a difference, it's like he's already part of our family.' Mum looked anxious. 'You will stay friends with him, Prue, when you start at Kingtown High?'

I sighed. 'I'll stay friends with him, Mum. *Just* friends, though.'

'Well, whatever you say, dear.' Mum beamed at me. 'It's good that your dad doesn't mind too much about you going to Kingtown, as he went there himself.'

I was starting there at the beginning of the spring term. Miss Wilmott had pulled strings to get me a place there. My dad's old grammar school. I wasn't at all sure how I was going to get on there. If I was so hopeless at so many subjects at a school like Wentworth then surely I'd be floundering helplessly at a school with high academic standards.

When I went to see the headteacher I found her surprisingly reassuring.

'I understand your blind spot when it comes to maths, Prudence. I'm not too bright at maths myself. We'll see about some extra tutoring in various subjects, but obviously you're a girl who's going to excel at the arts. Miss Wilmott sent us your entrance papers for Wentworth, saying she thought you'd be an excellent student at our school, if we could possibly find a place for you. Your Shakespeare essay was outstanding.'

Mum was giving me the full Kingtown uniform for Christmas, with leftover Reverend Knightly money. 'You need to get off to the right start this time,' she said. 'I'm sure you're going to be really happy at Kingtown, dear. I wonder what the art teacher will be like? I know you thought very highly of that Mr Raxberry at Wentworth.'

I said nothing, bending my head, hiding behind my hair.

'I think you maybe had a little crush on him,' said Mum.

I swallowed.

'It's all right, dear. It's all part of growing up. But you'll get over it soon enough.'

I knew Mum meant well, but she simply didn't understand. I knew I'd never be really happy again. I missed Rax so so much. I couldn't bear to be without him. Sometimes it was so overwhelming that I had to shut myself away and cry and cry. I thought about him first thing in the morning and last thing at night. I dreamed about him. I painted him over and over again. I wrote very long letters to him, though I tore each one into tiny shreds.

I lived my ordinary life, I coached Dad with his speech, I helped Mum in the shop, I fooled around with Grace, I chatted to Toby – but it was just like a play. I was saying all the right words, going through all the motions, but none of it seemed *real*. I was pretending all the time. I just wanted to see Rax, to talk to him, to throw my arms around his neck, to kiss him, to tell him just how much I loved him, and that I would go on loving him for ever and ever.

I stayed right away from Wentworth — but several times I couldn't stop myself getting the bus and walking along Laurel Grove. I paused outside number 34, but then I walked on. I walked and walked and walked, slowly, dreamily, as if I was strolling along the seashore . . .

ABOUT THE AUTHOR

JACQUELINE WILSON is one of Britain's most
outstanding writers for young readers. She is the
most borrowed author from British libraries and
has sold over 20 million books in this country.
As a child, she always wanted to be a writer
and wrote her first 'novel' when she was nine,
filling countless exercise books as she grew up.
She started work at a publishing company and
then went on to work as a journalist on *Jackie*
magazine (which was named after her) before
turning to writing fiction full-time.

Jacqueline has been honoured with many of the
UK's top awards for children's books, including
the Guardian Children's Fiction Award, the
Smarties Prize and the Children's Book of the
Year. She was awarded an OBE in 2002 and is
the Children's Laureate for 2005-2007.

'A brilliant writer of wit and subtlety whose
stories are never patronising and are often
complex and many-layered' *The Times*

'It's the combination of accessible stories
and humorous but penetrating treatment of
big emotional themes that makes this
writer so good' *Financial Times*

THE DIAMOND GIRLS

Jacqueline Wilson

*'You're all my favourite Diamond girls,' said Mum.
'Little sparkling gems, the lot of you . . .'*

Dixie, Rochelle, Jude and Martine – the
Diamond girls! They might sound like a girl band
but these sisters' lives are anything but glamorous.
They've moved into a terrible house on a run-down
estate and after barely five minutes Rochelle's
flirting, Jude's fighting and Martine's storming off.
Even though Dixie's the youngest, she's desperate
to get the house fixed up before Mum comes home
with her new baby. Will the Diamond girls pull
together in time for the first Diamond boy?

'A compelling mix of gritty realism and warmth
where the chaos is largely redeemed by love'
Independent

'Jacqueline Wilson is . . . a national treasure . . .
The Diamond Girls is a modern-day drama . . .
Moving stuff with lashings of humour'
Birmingham Post

'Wilson writes with such humour and affection
for her characters that this book is full of
unexpected joy' *Daily Mail*

ISBN 0 552 55376 X